I0595221

Anne Beale

Nothing Venture, Nothing Have

Vol. III

Anne Beale

Nothing Venture, Nothing Have
Vol. III

ISBN/EAN: 9783337040314

Printed in Europe, USA, Canada, Australia, Japan

Cover: Foto ©Andreas Hilbeck / pixelio.de

More available books at **www.hansebooks.com**

NOTHING VENTURE,

NOTHING HAVE.

A Novel.

BY ANNE BEALE,

AUTHOR OF "GLADYS THE REAPER," ETC.

IN THREE VOLUMES.

VOL. III.

LONDON:
RICHARD BENTLEY, NEW BURLINGTON STREET.
1864.

CONTENTS.

CONTENTS.

CHAPTER I.

KERN'S LOVERS.

WILLIAM EAGLES and Madam Rambully continued very ill. Each was making every effort to get away from Yeo, but each was kept in that quiet parish, by a weakness that they could not resist. Their fretting against the chain that held them, retarded their recovery. A burst blood-vessel, and a broken leg, are slow to heal and mend.

So Mr. Eagles and Ellen were put to great straits to keep their patient quiet, and Aline and Fluke were equally embarrassed in keeping theirs.

Meanwhile, Madam Rambully positively forbade Aline from having any intercourse whatever with the outer world. She was neither to meet Mrs. Bat nor Lachlan. She declared her resolution of going away from the Downs as soon as she could move, and until that period, Aline must be contented with her society, or cause her to be carried away, at the danger of her life. Aline yielded to her mother's orders, but at the cost of many secret tears.

It was hard to be forbidden the sight of the two friends she loved best in the world, just when she was in the greatest trouble she had ever known. However, she found constant occupation in waiting on her mother, who, blind and confined to her bed, became more than usually irritable and excitable.

While the farm and the Nest were thus troubled in their inmates, a new life began at the Downs Hall. That house was, at last, completed, and well filled with company. Sir John Nux had brought his mother and Kern Lyons to the Hall, from London, and when they had seen that the elegant furniture of his most elegant abode, was arranged in the most perfect taste, he began to call in his guests.

The Downs Hall was built in the Italian style of architecture. It shone like snow in sunshine, amongst the green trees and undulating lawns that surrounded it. So new, white, and graceful was the outside, that you guessed at the elegance of the interior before you entered it. Like its master, it all seemed framed for the enjoyment of the present moment.

As I said before, the house was filled with company. It matters not much to the course of this story, that there were " noble lords and ladies gay," country squires, and the usual amount of county visitors, coming and going from day to day, and week to week, during the autumn and winter. But it matters somewhat that Kern Lyons was the great centre of attraction to the men, and the great centre of envy and detraction to most of the women. I say most, because there are women who are superior to the low vice of jealousy. It matters, also, that Lachlan Lyons was occasionally invited to swell the guests at the dinner table, or to enjoy a day's sport in the manor that had once belonged to his forefathers.

Of course the Bats, Loves, Ravens, and Daws, had their regular invitations, by turns, and accepted or declined as they saw fit.

Ellen found herself launched, at once, amongst the " county society," and became a very popular ingredient in it. She and her husband might have lived at the Hall, had they been so inclined—but they preferred the quiet of home, and only accepted such invitations as they were bound to accept, all of which they duly returned.

Everybody found out that Kern's father was nothing more nor less than a respectable farmer. True, he was a Lyons, and looked a gentleman when he had on his best coat; true, his children were all well dressed, good-looking, and tolerably well educated—but he was a farmer to all intents and purposes, and the Manor Farm did not belong to him, but to the Misses Daw. Still, nobody ever could or ever did think of this when they were in Kern's society. She was a lady, a beauty, a genius, what was she not?

One day, towards the end of autumn, Kern either had, or feigned to have, a headache in the morning, and remained in her room to breakfast. She requested Lady Nux, as a favour, to let her stay in-doors the whole of that day, and to leave her alone until dinner.

She knew that the gentlemen were all going out shooting, and that the ladies were variously engaged out of doors, so she reckoned on having the morning to herself.

She betook herself to the book-room, a small and cheerful apartment, looking into a flower-garden, through large windows, opening from the ground. She sat down in an easy chair near the window, and took up a volume of the *Promessi Sposi*, which, however, soon dropped on her lap.

The last two years of foreign society and education had given the finishing touch, so to say, to this uncommon girl. It would be difficult to say in what she was outwardly improved, but improvement there was. The long curls which had left England with her, were now drawn into the braids of a newer fashion, one of which circled above her forehead like a crown. This seemed to give more decided outline to the features, and a more classic cast to the head. She had on a rich silk dress of that pale sea-green colour that contrasts so well with a complexion such as Kern's was. It was like the young green leaves to the blush rose-bud. The large open sleeves then worn, showed to the elbow an arm that had served as model to more than one Italian sculptor, and which, at that moment, supported her graceful head, as the elbow rested on an arm of the chair.

It is as impossible to give a just idea of her as it would be to describe the hues of morning, or the form of a perfect flower. She was now so accustomed to all the epithets that are lavished on beauty, that she was almost tired of them, and generally received them for what they were worth. But, of praise of her various talents and accomplishments, she was greedy still, and accordingly studied whenever she had the opportunity. She had realized the dream of her girlhood. "She had made all men love her, and all women jealous of her." That she was not much the happier for this consummation, we shall see, if we look into the thoughts that were passing in her mind. They were something as follows :

" I feel that I must decide before this winter is over. At once, indeed. And what am I to decide? If I marry the man I don't love, I shall have rank, position, riches,—if I sacrifice myself to the one I do love, I shall have poverty and insignificance. If I bring the one who is tolerably indifferent to me, to the point, as I may do, I shall have everything but an ancient family, and that is a *sine quâ non*. But he cares for nothing but my beauty and talents. He would marry me, because he sees every one else at my feet. Robert Love is really attached to me in his rough bullying way—and the rest are like wasps about honey, buzzing and sipping, because, I suppose, they think me sweet. And the one I could love—have loved—do love—has never had the courage to tell me that he loves me. Must I unwoman myself and make him confess? I must know the truth. But, even. then, I could not give up rank and wealth for love. Better to be a peer's wife without love, than a poor commoner's with it. Yet, I would give all I have to hear that one word which I have heard with contempt and indifference from others, from his lips. I see him watch me—he *must* love me. He alone of all this throng of adorers, is the only one who has never praised my beauty, or complimented me on my powers. He shall do so. I must hear the word—revel an hour in the consciousness of his attachment, and then crush it, and my own foolish fancy, under the golden weight of rank."

Kern had just come to this conclusion when she was startled by a footstep in the verandah. She got up to leave the room, but before she could do so Captain Love walked in through the window. That admirable young man was now captain, by purchase.

"I have caught you at last, Kern," he said, "and you are not going away. I watched all the pack off, and then, when I had the field to myself, I came up here. I thought I should find you in this room. Now, I've got you to myself, I mean to have it all out with you, and the sooner the better."

"I stayed at home because I was not well, and I really cannot talk," said Kern, languidly.

"By George, but you look better than I ever saw you in my life, and you may as well sit down. If you won't, I'll have it all out in public, I'll be hanged if I don't."

Bullying Bob looked so savage, that Kern thought it wisest to obey, so she sat down.

"I really do not see what you can have to say to me," she said.

"I dare say *you* don't, but *I* do. Now I won't go shilly shallying any longer. You've been making a fool of me these five or six years."

"Oh, you are mistaken, *I* did not make you a fool, Captain Love."

"You've made me dance after you in London, and over in that fandango of an Italy, and down here at Yeo, till I am tired of it. Now you must tell me here, at once, when you mean to have me. You know you've promised me a hundred times."

"I promised you! Oh! you are deceiving yourself. I could not promise, because you know you have nothing independent of your father, and those sweet Miss Daws, and the rest of them would not approve of me."

"I've offended my ugly old aunts, by nearly upsetting them in giving that vulgar upstart cousin of yours a hiding—I'll be the death of him yet?"

"Cousin? who? Lachlan?

"Yes. *Lackland*, by name and trade. He won't forget it."

"Oh! I should think not. He is a very small, weak, cowardly young man. I dare say he made no effort to return the compliment? You remember when you knighted him ?"

The Captain winced.

"That was all for your sake, too ; you were always 'running about after him."

"I! well, I scarcely think I am under the necessity of running about after men, especially my own cousin. But is this what you want with me ?"

"I want you to say downright yes or no, before I go away. By George, if you don't, I'll tell your father you promised to marry me, and ask his consent."

"He won't believe you, and won't give his consent. You have no proofs."

"Kern, you're deeper than any woman I ever saw in my life."

"You could not pay me a higher compliment. But I do not see how I have earned it."

"You've kept me in your snares ever since I was a boy: you've drawn in Nux, you've caught Inncaster."

"I think you may give his lordship his title."

"He hasn't much else to boast of. He's past sixty, he wears a wig, he's got false teeth, he's padded from head to foot. I believe he rouges, I know he's rheumatic or gouty—and yet you'll marry him because he's a lord."

"And why should I not if I have no objection to these things?"

Bullying Bob answered this question, by an oath, and by getting up from his seat and seizing Kern's arm somewhat roughly for a lover. Then he said—

"Because you've promised me—you know you have. You've as good as said you'd have me fifty times, and so you shall, or I'll——"

"You will be so good as to let me go," said Kern, coolly. "I have been used to *gentlemen* of late, and they do not pinch a lady's arm."

Bob flung down the arm with another oath.

"Yes, or No," he roared out.

There was another step in the verandah.

"Hush!" said Kern, "some one is coming."

"Some one be hanged!" said Bob.

"I sincerely hope that is not to be my fate," said a quiet, bland voice from without. "I beg your pardon. I was not listening intentionally. I did not know any one was here; Miss Lyons, I trust your head is better. I should scarcely think such loud words good for it—I will not intrude, only I·left some percussion caps here, and——"

"Pray come in, Lord Inncaster," said Kern, her cheek slightly flushed, "Captain Love was enthusiastic."

Lord Inncaster came into the room, as Bob scowled fiercely at Kern, and caught up his hat.

"Pray do not let me disturb so pleasant a conversation," said his lordship. "I am going as soon as I have found what I wanted."

"One moment, Lord Inncaster," said Kern. "This is the passage we were discussing. I was right, I think *Lucia* says just what I thought she did."   Lord Inncaster took the seat vacated by Bob.

"Good morning," growled Bob ; "I have an engagement at twelve."

"We can finish our conversation another time," said Kern. "You will be here this evening ?"

Bob disappeared through the open window.

"May I close this window ?" said Lord Inncaster.

He did so, and sat down again.

Lord Inncaster was, as Bob justly said, full

sixty years old, and had so fine a head of hair, that people invidiously said it was a wig. But he was a young-looking man for his years. If he padded, rouged, had false teeth, &c., it was all so well managed, that no one had a right to say so. He was an aristocratic-looking man. I wish I could find a less hackneyed word to express my meaning, but I cannot. Tall, pale, with marked features, and graceful figure, he was eminently a gentleman in appearance. He was so like Kern, that he might have been her father. His high forehead did not betoken intellect, neither was there any great expression in his cold grey eyes—still there was no deficiency of either. He looked a man of average ability, with a tolerable portion of pride and dignity in his bearing.

"Miss Lyons," he began, with some hesitation of voice and manner, "I have at last found the opportunity I have so long sought. When I saw you last in Italy, you told me that you wished to wait until you were twenty-one before you married. I yielded, because I could not help myself. But I have remained unmarried, as I said I should. Indeed how could any man think of any woman but you, having once seen you? I accepted Lady Nux's invitation to this place on your account. I must now beg for your final decision. I cannot long submit to seeing those insufferable young puppies buzzing about you from morning till night. Surely a young lady of your discretion could not——"

"My lord, I have given them no encouragement," said Kern.

"I must do you the justice to say you have not. But perhaps you do not discourage them. At all events, I am here to have my sentence pronounced."

"Your lordship is aware that my father lives near this place. He has not been consulted."

Kern's face flushed as she said this, and she threw a searching glance upon Lord Inncaster.

"I understand, from Lady Nux, that your father is scarcely now——I mean that you are your own mistress."

"You will perhaps allow me to consult my father. He is a proud man, although a fallen branch of an old family. You know that the baronetcy of which my cousin is the representative, is one of the oldest in England?"

Lord Inncaster bowed.

"I have no doubt but that my father will allow me to do as I like, and will feel honoured by your proposal—at least will feel that it is such as our family would have approved, in former days. Under his present fortunes, I think he would rather not see you himself."

"Precisely; that is just what I should wish. It is you, Miss Lyons, whom I seek, and I have always considered that relations had better keep out of the way until after marriage. They only do mischief. Lawyers are the only admissible interferers. If you like, my attorney shall negotiate."

Kern's lip curled.

"Thanks, Lord Inncaster. My father might not approve. I shall be the best negotiator."

"Then if you obtain your father's consent, which I look on as a mere matter of form, I may hope for my answer——"

"In three days at most," said Kern.

"And can you still affirm that the slight disparity in our ages would not prevent your returning the—the—adoration I feel for you."

"I say now, as before, that the only disparity I have been able to discover, is that of rank;

and even this is more nominal than real, since our family is——"

" Ah, yes! I really have never thought of your family. I do not even care to inquire whether you have a mother, a brother, or sister. You tell me you have a father; but this is indifferent. We shall live in London, in the North of England, where my property is —abroad—and cannot come into collision. *You* would grace a crown, much less a coronet."

Lord Inncaster took Kern's hand, and as he bent over it, did not see the look of haughty anger that flashed into her face for a moment. Still less could he read the thoughts beneath.

" He despises our family. I will not have him."

For a moment the proper pride overcame the false.

She rose under its influence.

" You will excuse me now, Lord Inncaster," she said; " my headaches always get worse when I am excited."

" You will remember your promise to put me out of this cruel suspense in three days," said his lordship.

" I shall have made up my own mind, and spoken to my father in three days," said Kern.

" Make up her mind?" repeated Lord Inncaster, as Kern walked majestically through the door, which his lordship held open for her. " Her own mind surely is settled long ago. I suppose she dislikes my not wishing to have anything to do with her family ; but of course that would be impossible. Even her queenly beauty and carriage could not be a sufficient set off for these agricultural descendants of the old Lyons family. They were well enough, perhaps ; but nobody knows what these may be, so I make up my mind not to inquire. But she will be obliged to keep these swarms of adorers off when she is Lady Inncaster. I never yet endured a rival, and could shoot them all with pleasure.

CHAPTER II.

KERN'S OFFERS.

THAT evening there was a large dinner party at the Hall, and Kern had lost her headache. She was even more stately, beautiful, and brilliant than usual.

" If I am to sell myself," she said, " I will show them all that I am worth buying."

Mr. and Mrs. Oliver Bat, Captain Love, junior, and Lachlan were amongst the guests.

Sir John Nux was a pleasant host, and made his house very agreeable. People liked him for his good nature, and laughed at his ancestry. The old county families had almost more respect for the memory of the Lyonses than for the riches of their successors. However, he was a baronet, and had plenty of money.

He admired Kern as much, or perhaps more, than any one else, but he had the happy power of transferring his affections from one beautiful object to another, so he had never actually proposed for her. Nobody could tell whether she liked him or not, but on this particular evening she seemed resolved to attract him. She sang his favourite songs, she talked to him of his beloved Italy, and flattered him in a way that she alone knew how to do. Lord Inncaster was jealous—Bullying Bob furious—and all the other young men disgusted, because it was impossible to get near that lovely Miss Lyons.

"I am so glad you have invited my cousin, Sir John," she said. "It is very kind of you. He is not really so *gauche* as one might expect."

"He is a very clever, gentlemanly fellow," said Sir John. "People say he will be a great engineer."

"Would you mind telling him that I want to send a message by him?" said Kern. "He keeps so entirely with the Bats that there is no getting at him. Do you remember Mrs. Bat before her marriage? I think her quite embellished."

"I was going to say that matrimony must embellish a woman, when I remembered that nothing could make Miss Kern Lyons more beautiful than she is. When are you going to take compassion on one of us pining adoratos?"

"When the right adorato asks me, I suppose," said Kern, looking straight at Sir John with her enigmatical eyes.

"I wish I could be vain enough to suppose it were I," sighed Sir John.

"Have you not said those words to French, English, Italian, Spanish, Portuguese, and, for aught I know, South-Sea Islanders?—for I believe some of them are beautiful," asked Kern.

"I never said them to mean them before," said Sir John.

"I should like to know what you *do* mean," said Kern.

"Miss Lyons, I am commissioned by Lady Nux to ask if you will assist in a charade," said Lord Inncaster, approaching.

"With pleasure," replied Kern, rising. "Will you give my message to my cousin, Sir John?"

"I will, and then come and help you in the charade."

Sir John went off; Lord Inncaster offered Kern his arm. Sir John looked round as they walked through the drawing-room into a saloon, and said to himself—

"Will she marry him? They are a handsome couple, in spite of his age. I would marry her to-morrow if I thought she really loved me; but I know no more of her heart now than I did when I first saw her; and it would be dreadfully dull work to tie oneself down yet for a few years, at least. I will watch the end of old Inncaster first, at any rate. Besides, as my mother says, it would be awkward to have her as mistress here, with all those other branches of her family on all sides of us.

Sir John reached Lachlan as he came to this conclusion. He gave him Kern's message.

"How cruel of you, Nux, to make Lord Inncaster so jealous," said Mr. Oliver Bat, who had been watching Kern half the evening.

"Will you come and help in a charade?" said Sir John in reply.

"No; but Lachlan will. He is capital at it. He did a whole Turkish one for us the other evening."

"Will you come?" asked Sir John; "and then your cousin can give you her message."

Lachlan went with Sir John, and, rather against his will, found himself amidst a party of young people, who were settling a charade in the library. Mrs. Oliver Bat was amongst them.

"Oh, Lachlan! I was just talking of you," she said. "He is capital. He is a first-rate actor."

"Quite a new accomplishment," said Kern.

It is unnecessary to enter into the various details of the charades. Kern, with her usual tact, refused to take the principal parts, but was so clever herself that every part she took became a principal one. To Lachlan, she managed to give the most conspicuous characters, and was surprised to find her "gauche" cousin her very best aid. Lachlan had a good voice, and what is called mobile features, so his first appearance on the Downs Hall stage was a great success. Lachlan suddenly became a hero amongst the ladies, and Mrs. Bat was delighted to answer various inquiries as to who he was.

"A cousin of Miss Lyons's and a nephew of the Miss Daws," was her unvarying reply.

"Where did you learn to make yourself of so much use?" asked Kern, during a pause in the charade.

"I don't call this being of use," said Lachlan.

"Well, making yourself agreeable?"

"I think it was on board ship," said Lachlan.

"Will you walk with me to-morrow across the fields to Jemima's?" asked Kern.

"I have only the afternoon free," said Lachlan.

"But I want your advice, and must see you. I will go at any hour."

"I can manage to be in the Hawthorn copse at three," said Lachlan. "I shall be surveying there. Or I will call here for you."

"No; I think I would rather meet you, and walk with you. At three then."

"Kern, what is the matter? you are not well."

"I am simply bored."

"How?"

"By men."

"Too many lovers! Oh Kern."

There was something so sad and reproachful

in Lachlan's voice, that Kern looked at him, and coloured.

"Have I done anything wrong?" she asked, sarcastically.

"I suppose it is the fault of beauty and talent, Kern," sighed Lachlan, and turned away, to answer some question put to him by Mr. Bat. Kern looked at him, and a triumphant smile lighted up her beautiful face.

"Yes, he loves me too," she thought, and the next moment she was entreating Miss Love to play the part of queen in a quickly-arranged charade, in which Lachlan and Sir John were the principal male characters.

"Excuse me," said Sir John, "you must be queen, Miss Lyons. Mrs. Bat and I have arranged it all; you shall be Mary Stuart; your cousin will make a capital Darnley; I will be Rizzio; and we can have murderers *ad libitum.*"

Sir John had his way, and a scene was soon improvised, of which Kern was the prominent figure.

In five minutes she had transformed herself into a Mary Stuart. A train of black velvet added to her white dress, and the little three-cornered lace head-dress, were all she wanted to make the likeness perfect. The charade was "assassination," and this was the last act.

Scene.—Kern, as Mary Stuart, reclining on a sofa; Sir John, as Rizzio, singing to a guitar, "Mary, Mary, queen of my soul." Enter, Lachlan, as Darnley, with followers, and assassinates Rizzio.

Kern's acting was, like everything else she did, perfect. The grace with which she received Rizzio's adoration was only surpassed by the agony at his murder. When she threw herself between him and Darnley, fell on her knees before the one, and shielded the other with her arm, and finally sank, fainting, on the floor when her appeal proved in vain, she showed a real dramatic power.

The applause of the spectators was as great as if it had been a scene on the stage.

"It was Mary Stuart herself," said Ellen Bat, suddenly recollecting a scene of a bygone day, when Kern had said to her and Aline, that she wished she could, like the unfortunate Mary, "make all men love, and all women hate her."

"Yes," said Miss Love, sarcastically, " it

seems a pity she doesn't turn her talents to account, and go upon the stage."

"She'd beat Grisi hollow," said Bullying Bob.

" And elevate her position and herself," said Mr. Oliver.

"She would adorn any position," said Lord Inncaster.

While these and similar remarks were making among the audience, the actors were enacting another scene, quite impromptu, behind the scenes.

Sir John was proposing for Kern Lyons. Rizzio was actually daring to make an offer to Mary Stuart.

Sir John never knew what it was that made him so suddenly resolve to do the fatal deed. But he did it, then and there, just after he had helped Kern to rise from the floor after her feigned swoon.

Kern, ever mistress of herself, heard the hurried words, and saw the emotion of the speaker with a keen thrill of pleasure.

"Miss Lyons, every word I said to you as Rizzio, I feel and mean in my own person.   If you have a heart, tell me, at once, if I may claim it."

Some such words as these, Kern heard, and a gleam of triumph shot through her impenetrable eyes.

"Why so sudden, Sir John? You startle me," said Kern, looking anything but startled.

"Because I see so many lovers fluttering round you. Now your cousin is added to the list."

"Ah!" exclaimed Kern, a genuine flush mounting to her cheeks, as she glanced round.

"He is gone," said Sir John. "We are alone for the moment. You *must* tell me, is it to be the ancient earl, the bullying ensign, the plodding engineer, any of the thousand and one in London or abroad, or may I venture to hope?"

"You are not serious, Sir John."

"Do you suppose I cannot love, that you persist in doubting me?"

"Excuse me, but you have loved so many— I must be pardoned for wishing to feel quite certain that the butterfly is caught at last."

"Oh Kern! Kern! why were you ever so gifted, and yet so heartless?"

"Not heartless, Sir John; I think I could give a heart in return for one that I believed wholly mine."

"And you do not believe mine to be yours?"

"I will tell you in three days, when I have watched your flutterings about other flowers, and your flights towards the Downs farm, after that hidden violet, Aline."

"*Ce n'est que pour passer le temps.* I forget the minor flowers in presence of the queen rose. You are the Mary Stuart, the rose, the pearl of women, and you know it, Kern. All the other stars pale before you."

"In three days, Sir John," said Kern, pointing quickly to the door.

"Mary Stuart recovered from her swoon, and Rizzio come to life again," said Lord Inncaster, who entered the saloon, followed by some of the other guests.

"I believe they are rehearsing for a future charade," said Miss Love.

"Oh no!" said Kern, "we were merely going over the last scene in a different way, to see which was best—the song or a dialogue."

"You are a finished actress at any rate," muttered Sir John, as Kern turned to speak to Lord Inncaster.

The actors were duly praised, and when Lachlan was called for to receive his ovation,

Lady Nux said that he had left. He had begged her to apologize to Sir John, and to say that he had an early engagement the following morning, which must be his excuse for going away so soon.

Kern frowned slightly. Had he heard Sir John's proposal?

Kern needed her utmost tact to manage her lovers during the remainder of that evening. The most impracticable of them was Bob, who never came across her without upbraiding her.

"You are playing at fast and loose with me, you know you are. If you throw me over for old Inncaster, I vow I'll expose you. You know you have as good as promised to have me a hundred times, and I'll blow my brains out if you don't."

"Be quite sure you have brains to blow, before you make the attempt," was Kern's rejoinder.

"Then I'll blow cousin Lachlan's brains out," said Bob, scowling ominously. "You'll allow he's got a few."

"Certainly," said Kern, "but they are likely to do him good service for many a long year to come."

"I'm a pretty good shot, if I'm nothing else," growled Bob, turning away. "Good night, Kern; I'm not going to stay here to be a foil, anyhow."

So saying he left the party abruptly.

Kern told Lady Nux that evening that she was obliged to go home for two days, and should do so on the morrow. Lady Nux, who had been quite alive to her son's especial devotion, did not make her usual objections, but simply asked Kern if she had, at last, made up her mind to accept or decline Lord Inncaster's proposals. Kern said that she intended to come to some final decision at once, and therefore wished to consult her relations. Lady Nux said she really did not know how they would get on without her, which was true; and so they separated for the night.

CHAPTER III.

KERN'S DECISION.

LACHLAN kept his appointment on the morrow, and he and Kern walked together to the Squoire's. Kern had not been to Brooklands since she had been in the country, and Jemima and George were very indignant.

It was just such a day in October, as that on which Ellen Eagles was married, and instinctively, each of them thought of that day. As they walked through the brown, yellow, rustly, crisp leaves that had fallen from the trees of the Downs Hall woods, they were reminded of similar leaves that strewed the paths on that auspicious occasion. The shadows and sunbeams that flickered before them, and the red-brown of the soil, seemed a portion of that particular period of their lives. Kern said that she could not help thinking of Mrs. Bat's wedding-day, and Lachlan confessed to similar thoughts. Kern said that it was a very long time since they had walked alone together, and that doing so recalled a great many scenes of their past lives. For once there was a tone of sentiment in Kern, which Lachlan had rarely, if ever, heard before. Her conversation was as fitful as her varying colour, or as the lights and shadows playing among the trees. Lachlan, too, was grave and silent, waiting for the confidence he expected from Kern.

As she walked by his side, scarcely to all appearance shorter than himself, and he was above six feet in height, he was thinking of the time when, boy and girl together, she had so often told him of her determination to be a great lady. The noble lover of the previous evening—the swarms of lovers, in short—came before his mind, and he saw that the dreams of the Kern Lyons of the Manor Farm were likely to be realized in the majestic girl that was by his side. His dreams, too, of professional eminence and usefulness were no longer entirely visionary, and the last ten years had been years of great and momentous changes to both.

When they emerged from the woods, they came out into open meadows that led from the Downs Hall to Brooklands, and belonged partly to Sir John and partly to the Squoire. The river Yeo, and its tributary the brook, flowed through these meadows, and it was by the banks of the latter that they walked for a mile or two.

"Do you remember that first walk of ours, over the downs, and by the brook, to my grandfather's, cousin?" asked Kern.

The old, familiar term, "cousin," had not passed Kern's lips in addressing Lachlan for years.

"I remember it almost better than any scene of my life," said Lachlan.

He thought of that sweet child, Aline, who had met them in the farm-yard, with kind words and dirty pinafore—of Fluke and her scolding—and of the blind, expectant mother.

"Cousin," said Kern, abruptly, her face flushing like the autumn sky, "I want your advice. You have seen more of the world than my father or brothers, and therefore I appeal to you."

"You shall have such advice as a brother

can give," said Lachlan ; "for have we not always been as brother and sister ?"

"No," said Kern, impatiently.

"No," echoed Lachlan, as he remembered when she feigned not to recognize him in his navvy dress.

"I had two serious proposals of marriage yesterday, in addition to one always being repeated," said Kern.

"I suspected as much, cousin. I fancied from Lord Inncaster's manner that he had made you an offer, and I left the saloon at the hall, to avoid being an eaves-dropper to what Sir John was beginning to say."

"And you never hinted your suspicions to me, Lachlan ?"

"You never made me a confidant, cousin. I should not have ventured to pry into your secrets."

"Secrets !" exclaimed Kern, half reproachfully. "If you cared—Well. I have promised to make up my mind in three days, and I want your advice. Here are a peer and a baronet at the feet of your humble cousin, *née* Kern Lyons, of the Manor Farm. Which shall I have ?"

" Which do you love ?"

" Neither."

" Then marry neither."

" Why ?"

" Because without love there can be no happiness."

" Don't you believe in that 'esteem,' and 'love after marriage,' that grandmothers and maiden aunts tell us of?"

" Certainly not."

" Then you would never marry for fortune, or family, or position ?"

" If I knew myself I would not."

Kern was silent for a few minutes, and then said suddenly, casting a searching glance at Lachlan—

" Lachlan, were you ever in love ?"

Lachlan coloured like a girl at the question, but answered steadily—

" Yes," returning Kern's glance.

Her eyes looked down at once.

" What do you think of Lord Inncaster ?" she said.

" He is an earl and a gentleman, but too old for you; unless, indeed, all that you desire is to be a countess, and then he would be as well as another."

" And of Sir John Nux ?"

" I should think most ladies might find him agreeable ; and he is certainly of a suitable age. I have often fancied you really cared for him. At all events you have given him encouragement."

" Encouragement! What a curious word. Does the rose encourage the butterfly ?"

" Kern, you are such an enigma that I fail to read your meaning."

" Blind and deaf!" muttered Kern, in answer to this. " Is not the rose simply passive when she receives the visit of the butterfly, and does she not long for the devotion of the lark, or the nightingale, or even the songless hawk, who soars above her? I am sure she does— she must."

" Why ?" asked Lachlan. " Are women all so ambitious ?"

" Every woman longs for the love of the creature she loves, I suppose," said Kern, half indifferently, half suggestively.

" But surely you, cousin, can command what you desire."

" Can I? Prove it. Help me to it. Give it me You alone can. You think me a heartless coquette: you misjudge me: you have no sympathy with me, although you know that I can understand all your aspirations better than any one else in the world. We are both ambitious, the difference between us is only in name and in kind."

"Kern, I well know your powers, your beauty, your talents, and manifold attractions. They far surpass anything I possess. I valued them as soon as I knew you."

"If I am a riddle to you, Lachlan, you are one to me. I would give the world to read your heart."

Lachlan looked surprised, and coloured again. Kern misinterpreted his manner.

"You have caused me more anxiety and suspense than any other human being," she added, forgetting herself, and standing still near a stile which they had to cross.

They were within sight of the smoke from the chimneys of Brooklands, as it rose amongst the trees that flanked the house.

"I can bear it no longer. You will not speak—I must. Do you wish me to marry either of those men? I who can command the love, the devotion, of every man I see, cannot even make you,—my cousin,—my friend,—my childhood's companion,—my—my——"

Kern burst into tears.

Lachlan had never seen her shed tears before. What did she want?—what did she mean?

"My dear cousin—my dear Kern," he said, putting his hand affectionately on her shoulder, "what can I say or do? What makes you unhappy? Do not marry any man you cannot love. Are you attached to any one else? Do you—can I——"

"I do—you can—" sobbed Kern. "You know—you ought to know—that I have always loved you best."

Lachlan was not conceited or vain. He did not yet understand his cousin. The "best" referred, in his mind, to cousinly or brotherly feelings.

"Not better than your own brothers, Kern, or you could not have passed me as a stranger in a London street, because I wore a navvy's dress."

Kern flushed crimson.

"When? How?" she stammered.

"You know when, and how, cousin Kern," said Lachlan.

"That was the pride and vanity of eighteen," said Kern, getting hastily over the stile, to cover her momentary confusion, and walking rapidly onwards.

A sudden shower of rain obliged her to run as fast as she could across the last remaining meadow to the farm, and thus caused the conversation to cease.

When they reached the house, they learnt that George and the Squoire and Jemima were gone to a harvest home at the Downs, but that Kezia was expected shortly.

They went into the large, old-fashioned parlour, the pride of Jemima and her mother. Here was a large bow-window looking into a flower-garden, and a glass door opening into the same. Here were also carved oak chairs, tables, and cabinets, of great value, which had been heirlooms in the Squoire's family for generations.

Kern took off her bonnet and shawl, and sat down in the bow-window seat.

"I am glad they are all out," she said; "now we can finish our conversation. Lachlan, I have bitterly repented that one act of unkindness. How could you treasure it up, and repeat it as you did just now?"

"Because I have never since believed that you had any real affection for me."

"How little any one knows me. Lachlan, we must end this cruel mockery of silence. You believed in my affection up to that moment?"

"Yes."

"Then believe in it still. Why cannot you?"

"Because grand society, foreign manners, flattery, beauty, accomplishments — ambition and temptations, perhaps—have made of my Cousin Kern the fine lady she wished always to be : and placed her far above the Lachlan Lyons of her childhood."

"But have only strengthened and increased her old love for that Australian cousin. Oh! Lachlan! in spite of all my ambition—my pride—my grandeur—my—my—whatever you choose to call it—I have never ceased to love you since that day when you, Sir Lachlan Lyons, sat down on the turf above our old home, and cried like a girl. Then, as now, you and the old title were my truest, purest ambition."

Kern Lyons looked up at her cousin, who stood near her. For once her eyes were perfectly intelligible. For once there was timidity in the glance, usually so quietly assured. Lachlan could doubt no longer. The consciousness came to him that his cousin loved him, as he loved Aline; and it brought a great pain to his heart. This great pain must have given a corresponding expression to his ever legible countenance, every letter of which Kern had studied but too well. She read it in a moment. She grew red, then pale. She covered her face with her hands.

"Kern—my dear, dear cousin," was all Lachlan could say, as he put his hand on her bending head.

Kern remained for a few minutes in the attitude above described. She was trying to suppress some strong emotion, and she succeeded. She rose from her seat, pushed Lachlan's hand from her head, and stood before him. the Kern Lyons of everyday life, pale, calm, haughty, incomprehensible.

"Cousin," she said, laying a slight stress on the words, "you will kindly forget that I have paid you the greatest compliment that I ever paid to man, and such as I shall never pay again."

Lachlan felt like a culprit before the lovely woman whose love he had, tacitly, refused.

"Kern," he said, hesitating between every sentence, "you misunderstand yourself and me. We do not understand one another."

"Then, before we part, we had better understand one another. I have confessed to you the one weakness of my life. I have un-womaned myself. I saw that you understood me *at last*, idiot that I was to persist in enlightening you. You are a man, and, to a certain extent, a gentleman, you will forget what I have said."

An expression of irony passed over her features, as she said, "to a certain extent;" she was trying to avenge herself.

"Whether a gentleman or not, I hope I am a man of honour, cousin, and whatever concerns you is as dear to me as my own life."

Kern's lips quivered slightly.

"Then whom do you love better than her whose honour is dear to you as life?"

The ironical tone increased. Lachlan did not answer.

"Do I know my rival? Mine!"

Kern threw back her beautiful head, and

looked proudly into an old-fashioned looking glass, that hung in its carved oak frame, just opposite to where she stood.

"Kern," at last Lachlan said, sadly and gently, "do not humble yourself and me by such words as these. You and I have loved one another as brother and sister nearly ever since we met. But your sphere of life and mine are as far removed as the tropics from the poles. To-morrow, when you reflect on these few idle words, thrown out to prove your ungallant cousin, you will acknowledge that they are so. Mine is a hard-working, waiting life; yours is, and must be, one of power, and splendour. We will both forget this afternoon."

"Forget!" muttered Kern. "Lachlan, I thought you had a heart—and you—you thought that I had none!"

It was true, until that hour Lachlan had believed his cousin heartless.

"Kern, even in the sense you take it in, I have a heart. I have loved Aline and you for many years—but you were my cousin—my sister,—and Aline——"

"Aline!" shrieked Kern, suddenly forgetting herself, and thrown quite off her guard. "Do not say that you love Aline! that small, power-less, aimless child! am I always to be supplanted by her? In the affections of those who knew me first and best, *she* has stepped in before me. Mr. Eagles, Ellen, my own grandfather and grandmother, even my own sisters—but not you! oh not you, Lachlan Lyons! You, who were born for great deeds, could not love that silly, simple baby, Aline!"

"I could and do, Cousin Kern."

Lachlan could have borne any reproach di-rected against himself, but not words spoken slightingly of Aline.

"I love the girl who has been *your* friend for many years; whose education enabled you to be what you now are; who thinks you peerless in beauty and talent; who would not utter one reproachful word against you or any one else; and who is the sweetest and purest creature that ever trod this corrupt earth."

"I pity you, Lachlan," said Kern. "Aline may be too pure and sweet for this corrupt earth, but she is not worthy of you. She will not help you to be grand and great, poor silly child. She thinks of nothing but birds and flowers, and the farm-yard. Aline! an unknown, nameless, soulless girl, with big round black eyes like a doll's, and of whom, even now, no one knows anything. She may be——"

"Stop Kern," said Lachlan, authoritatively. "If you were a man, I would——"

"Knock me down," said Kern, recoiling beneath the stern, loud voice, and flashing eyes of her cousin.

Kern knew that Lachlan was not to be trifled with when excited. His grey orbs looked threateningly out from beneath their bushy brows. Still she was too angry herself to yield. She made him a sweeping curtsey, and receded before him, as he instinctively advanced towards her.

"Good day to you, Sir Lachlan," she said, sarcastically. "When next we meet I shall probably be Countess of Inncaster."

"Then," said Lachlan, bitterly, "you will, indeed, crush us all beneath the scornful tread of your feet."

Kern was at the door. She looked back with another sarcasm on her lips. There was something in Lachlan's face that stayed it. It was a strange mixture of severity and pity.

She turned—paused—then, with a sharp

cry fell down on her knees where she stood, saying—

"Lachlan, forgive me—pity me—let us part as friends, as cousins. We may never meet again."

Lachlan's temporary anger vanished in a moment. He hastened to Kern, and raised her from the ground. She was sobbing as if her heart would break—that heart, loosened from its life-long bands of pride and ambition.

Do not think, oh reader, that Lachlan was false in thought, word, or deed to Aline, because he put his arm tenderly round his cousin, and kissed her flushed cheek more than once. King Arthur was not purer or truer to Guinever, than he was to Aline, although he let Kern cling to him as she had never clung before, and never would again. At last she ceased to sob, and without looking at Lachlan, again withdrew to the door, saying—

"You must go, Lachlan; you must forget this afternoon. Try to think kindly of me, in spite of this. Go away before they come home: now at once; I would rather be alone."

Kern left the room. Lachlan stood some time thinking of his cousin in love and sorrow. Who and what was he to have gained the affections of such a woman? The knowledge humbled him. At first he longed to go after her and tell her so, and comfort her in some way or other; but this he knew would only renew the difficulty and danger of the past scene, so he followed her commands and left the farm.

He met Kezia, and with a hasty salutation, told her to go to Kern.

She did so, and found her in one of the bedrooms crying hysterically.

Kezia, the general comforter, put her arms round her, kissed her, spoke tenderly to her, but did not ask what ailed her. She had always known of Kern's love for Lachlan, and with sisterly love for both, had wished that it could be returned; but she had also discovered that Lachlan was attached to Aline, and had hoped that Kern's ambition would overcome the softer feeling. Now she guessed that some sort of explanation had taken place.

She had never seen Kern give way to any strong emotion before, and now she was frightened at her impetuosity. As she lay on the bed, with her face buried in the pillows, and her frame convulsed with sobs, she could scarcely believe her to be her proud sister.

"Kern, darling, compose yourself," she said, after waiting long.

"Compose myself!" said Kern, starting up; "I hate myself, I have disgraced myself, I shall never look him in the face again. I forget—you do not know——"

"I think I know, dear Kern. You may trust me."

"Then was it so evident," said Kern, "that you, and Bullying Bob, and even that wretch Aline should know it?"

"Only I, be sure, dear Kern. But do not call that sweet Aline by such a name."

"I hate her," said Kern, and the words seemed to do her good, and to recal her to herself.

Kezia shuddered.

"Do not preach, Kezia. I have much to do, and will do it, be assured. To-night I must go to bed, and try to forget this day,—I *will* forget it."

Kern got up, and walked across the room. She looked very pale, and her eyes were red with weeping.

"When will they be home, Kezia?"

"Not till late, I think."

"So much the better. I may sleep with

you. We have not slept together for many years."

There was a touch of feeling in Kern's voice when she said this. Tears came into Kezia's eyes.

" Oh Kern, if you had never——"

"I know what you mean, Kezia.   When this weakness is over, all will be well; my lot is decided for me now, and to-morrow I shall be glad that it is so.   I was not born to be rejected, was I ?"

For a moment Kern was grand and dignified, but tears came again, and the woman conquered.

" Let me go to your room.   A night's rest will be good.   I am very weary.   My head aches."

Kezia went with her to her bedroom; undressed her, made her some tea, tried to comfort her, and finally left her to herself.

Restless and unhappy, Kern lay long awake, thinking—thinking.   Before she fell asleep her fate was decided by herself.   She had resolved to become Countess of Inncaster.

CHAPTER IV

THE HARVEST-HUOME.

LACHLAN had promised Mr. Bull to be at the harvest home that evening.   Much against his will he fulfilled his promise.   As he walked hastily across the fields to the Downs Farm his mind was ill at ease.   He thought of Kern and Aline, and of both with sorrow. The former he had seen only too lately for their mutual peace, the latter he had not seen for weeks.   So carefully had she seemed to avoid all intercourse with him, that he was beginning even to mistrust her affection, and in spite of hard work and many good friends, felt jealous and unhappy.   He was not of a sentimental nature, but his love for Aline was deep and genuine, and he dreaded lest a shadow of doubt should come between them.

Almost nightly after his day's labour had he walked several miles upon the chance of seeing her, but in vain. She never came into the hall at the Downs when he was there, and he would leave the farm to stand in the late evening beneath her window in the faint hope of seeing at least her shadow cross it, or the light of her candle flicker behind its curtain.

When he reached the farm, the hall and kitchen were filled with joyous guests. The last load of corn had been carried, and master and men could well afford to rejoice. All the family of the Manor, as well as that at Brooklands, were helping to do honour to their father and their grandfather on this occasion. Plenty and good-humour crowned the board, and when Lachlan entered the house, he heard the following song being lustily sung by George Low, and the chorus joined in by every one present :—

"The groun' is clear, ther's nar a ear
  O' stannen carn a-left out now,
 Var win' to blow, ar râin to drow ;
  'Tis all up siafe in barn or mow.
 Here's health to thae that plough'd and zow'd ;
 Here's health to thae that reap'd and mow'd,

And thae that had to pitch a luoad,
Ar tip the rick at harvest-huome.
The happy zight—the merry night—
The men's delight—the harvest-huome.

" An' mid noo harm o' vire ar starm,
   Beval the farmer ar his carn,
An' ev'ry zack o' zeed gi'e back
   A hundred-vuold so much in barn.
And mid his Miaker bless his store,
His wife an' all that she've a-bore,
An' keep all evil out o' door,
Vrom harvest-huome to harvest-huome.
The happy zight—the merry night—
The men's delight—the harvest-huome."*

While these and many more similar verses
were sung by George and his uproarious chorus,
Lachlan 'stood in the doorway, unseen by the
singers, not liking to go into the hall until the
song was finished. But he was able to see
although he was not seen. There were farmer
and Mrs. Bull at the top and bottom of the
long table in the hall, with George and
Jemima, their two stout little boys, Esau,
Jacob, and Rhoda, to support them. Labourers
and their wives surrounded the table. In the

---

* From Mr. Barnes's " Poems of Rural Life in the Dorset
Dialect."

large kitchen, which could be seen through the door that opened into it from the hall, were Mr. and Mrs. Lyons, presiding at another long table, also filled with gay-hearted harvesters.

The roofs of both rooms rang with the chorus, and echoed again to the cheers that succeeded, as the healths of Mr. and Mrs. Bull and their respected family were drunk.

Just at this moment a light step was heard on the stairs, and Lachlan's heart told him Aline was coming. It told him true. Mrs. Fluke, who had made one of the harvest-home party during the first part of the evening, had gone upstairs to assure her mistress that Lachlan was not there, and to beg that Aline might, as was her custom, go down to hear the songs and healths. After some demur, Madam Rambully had consented.

"Aline," said Lachlan, leaving the door to meet her in the passage, "I see you at last."

He took both her hands in his, before she knew what he was doing, and looked into her eyes.

"All is right," he said, "I see. No change in you, my Aline. Why have you shunned me so?"

"Lachlan, I must not speak to you—I must not meet you. I have promised mamma not to see you, but you know I cannot change."

Big tears came into Aline's eyes.

"She has no right to prevent our meeting, Aline. Why will you not let me be your protector for life?"

"It cannot be, Lachlan; not now, at least. Mamma is very ill. I can never leave her, and I cannot vex her. I am very deceitful to speak to you now."

Aline was moving away; Lachlan detained her.

"Aline, I am going away soon. Are we not to meet again, not to write to one another?"

"We shall hear of each other, Lachlan, but I must not write. But, oh! do not go away from me, I am so very, very lonely."

The tears flowed faster. Lachlan saw that Aline's face was very pale, and her sweet eyes looked dim.

"Aline, I must see you again. I will, in spite of your mother."

"No—no—dear Lachlan. I will ask her to let me see you once before you go away—if

you must go. And I will never forget you—
never, never!"

Aline brushed the tears from her eyes, and
went into the hall. She slipped into the
chimney-corner, where the Squoire was smok-
ing his pipe, and sat down almost unper-
ceived. Lachlan, after a minute's deliberation,
followed.

"Dree cheers for Measter Lachlan—Measter
Lachlan's health," resounded through the
room, as he entered it. He seemed to hear
and see no one but Aline.

"Better late than never," said farmer Bull.
"No song no supper."

Lachlan went round the tables in the two
rooms to shake hands with one and another
whom he had not chanced to see since he had
been in the country.

"Glad to zee 'e huome agen,' said one.

"Bee'st taller than measter, now," said a
second.

"How he've a growed! Navvy work's a
muost as good as vield work," a third.

"Spose you'll be looking out for Mrs. Lachlan zoon," a fourth.

"Lackadaisy! it be'ant but t'other day he

coom here from vurrin pearts ; it makes one veel old like, don't it ma'am, to zee the young volk grow up. Hem didn't mark var to be so tall."

This was addressed by one of the women to Mrs. Lyons.

" Yes, Polly, he's a fine young man," said Mrs. Lyons. " Just like my poor Matthew. I shall never live to see him again, with all the wear and tear I have to go through. He might have been here to-night, but for—"

" But for good luck, aunt," returned Lachlan. " Why, hasn't Matthew made his fortune, and married a nice wife, and done five thousand times better than he could have done at home? Let us drink his health. My cousin Matthew's health."

Lachlan roared his toast out at the top of his voice, and in a moment it resounded through the two rooms, with cheers so loud that the very barton rang with them.

" What did you do with Kern ?" asked Mr. Lyons, as Lachlan stood by his side while the cheering was going on.

" Left her at Brooklands with Kezia," said Lachlan, with an uneasy twitch of conscience.

"Too grand to come here, of course. What is to be the end of all this?"

"Marriage, I should think," said Lachlan.

"With some one who'll be ashamed of her relations; I wish I'd never let her go away."

When Lachlan had made the tour of the rooms, he found himself in the chimney-corner, by the side of Aline. While the toasts and singing were drowning the general hearing, Aline said to Lachlan, whose ears were keen enough for every word of hers—

"Lachlan, I will see you before you go away. I have made up my mind to tell mamma that I will do so. I think you had better come here some afternoon next week, and send word to me by granny that you are here, and I will come down. I shall tell granny the truth, that I wish to bid you good-bye."

"And Fluke?" suggested Lachlan, who did not quite like this matter-of-fact proceeding.

"I am nearly emancipated from poor Fluke, now," said Aline, smiling sadly. "I have been obliged to be very decided with poor old Fluke."

"Better not "—puff, puff. " Sensible, secret "—puff—" woman "—puff, puff.

Lachlan and Aline were not aware that the Squoire had such keen ears. He had heard their little confidences.

" Thank you, Mr. Low," said Aline, blushing. " She is, indeed a most excellent friend. Goodnight. I will go now without disturbing any one."

Aline shook hands with the Squoire and Lachlan, and slipped away, and so the light of the harvest home went out to Lachlan.

" Go in "—puff, puff—" and win,"—puff, winked the Squoire.

" He sees everything," said Lachlan to himself.

" Dree cheers for Madam and Miss," echoed through the room as Aline left it; "and dree for Mrs. Fluke," were added, as that lady entered and took her place.

Lachlan soon made an excuse of a long walk to the Royal Oak for leaving the party.

" Fine young "—puff—" man,"—puff; said the Squoire to Fluke, pointing after Lachlan with his pipe.

" Not very genteel!" said Mrs. Fluke.

" You be "—puff, puff—" uppish,"—puff.

" Perhaps so, sir! I'm used to gentle-folks."

" Any objection " — puff — " to gentlemen farmers ?" puff, puff.

" Certainly not, sir; they're next to the county gentry."

" Better "—puff—" a deal "—puff, puff— " than some o' them. Money in purse "—puff,— " and hay in rack,"—puff, puff,—" and corn in barn."

This was one of the longest sentences Mrs. Fluke had ever heard the Squoire utter.

" A most excellent man is a Dorsetshire yeoman, I'm sure, sir," said Fluke.

" Like one, yourself ?"—no puff. The Squoire laid his pipe on his knee for a minute, and looked up in Mrs. Fluke's face.

" Caun't say I should, sir," said the imperturbable Fluke.

" Better try,"—puff, puff. " I'll have you !" —puff. " You'll have I," puff; " haw, haw— there's a rhyme."

" Glad you're amused, sir."

" Mean it. Marry you,"—puff, puff. " Say yes, or no !"

"No, sir; much obleeged. *Very* much obleeged. I'm sure you're my sincere friend, but I've made up my mind never to marry, and I'm one that can live without a man, thank goodness. You're the quietest gentleman I've ever seen, and if I was to change my intention in favour of any one, you're the man—but I never will, sir; never!"

"Honour you,"—puff, puff. "Sorry,"—puff. "All for the best,"—puff, puff, puff. "Mima and George wouldn't,"—puff.

"To be sure not, sir; they would *not* like it at all; and quite natural. I shouldn't like a stepmother, and I'm sure you wouldn't."

"Haw, haw! think not"—puff; "shake hands. Friends, eh?"—puff, puff.

"For ever, sir. I say again, I'm greatly obleeged to you. A woman likes the honour of an offer, even if she don't find it convenient to accept it. And though I'm not one to make a boast of my offers (I've had several, sir, though you mayn't suppose it), I'm proud of yours, and shall feel it to my dying day."

"Shake hands," said the Squoire, again laying down his pipe. "Friends for life!"

While Fluke and the Squoire are shaking hands, and while the mirth and the songs, and the toasts get more and more uproarious, Lachlan, contrary to his determination, is loitering outside the house, underneath a certain window, watching for a light, or a shadow, or both.

Very beautiful is the September night. The broad, red-faced harvest-moon is rising behind the downs, and sheds her rays on them, and on the thatched roofs and gables of the farm. Amid the shadows of the high elms, poplar, ashes, and willows, the little brook flows on, ever singing its tender lullaby to the birds and cattle. Under these trees, and by this murmuring, musical, melancholy brook, Lachlan stands in shadow. He has stood there so often that the little brook knows him well, and sometimes shimmers under the moonbeams as if to bid him welcome. The nightingales, too, occasionally pour out their floods of music, as if, like fractious infants, no brooklet's lullaby could give them rest.

Lachlan was thinking of a letter he had received the previous day from Mr. Markman, offering him a very important post, as engineer in Russia, in a great work which he was about to undertake for the Russian government. This was to give Lachlan both fame and money, and might raise him to the top of his profession. These were indeed temptations: but how was he to leave Aline?

These thoughts were suddenly interrupted by the rustle of bushes behind him, and the sound of a low voice. Lachlan turned round, and found himself face to face with William Eagles.

A pale, spectral-looking man he was, and Lachlan could almost have believed him a ghost, as he stood amidst the shadows of the trees, through which a ray of moonlight fell, and made his ghastly face more ghastly still.

" What are you doing here, Lachlan Lyons ?" he said, in a harsh, angry voice.

" I ask you the same question," said Lachlan.

" By heavens, young man, if you don't leave this spot, and promise never again to think of that angel in yonder room, I'll shoot you."

Lachlan saw that he held something in his hand, and fearing that it might be a pistol, stepped aside. He had long believed that

William Eagles was subject to temporary fits of insanity, and prepared himself for a struggle.

"Mr. Eagles, if you love the angel you venture to name, lay down that weapon. It would kill her and her mother if a crime were done here. And you don't wish to commit three murders, if you do one."

As Lachlan spoke he moved, so as to have his hand ready to lay hold of the hand that held the pistol, if pistol it was.

"Kill them? No! It is you, who haunt their sacred shrine, that I want to kill. How dare you come here?"

"Give me that weapon, or throw it away, and I will tell you. I saved you from death once, now I will save you from sin. I have twenty times your strength, so it is useless to resist me."

William Eagles glanced at the tall, powerful, young man before him, and knew that he was right. But there was something wild and deadly in his large black eyes, and Lachlan did not feel sure of him.

"Look there," he said, "there she is—your good angel and mine."

William Eagles glanced towards the window

of Aline's bedroom, and there, looking out upon the calm night through the casement that she had opened, was Aline. Her sweet, pale face, and the white sleeve of her dress, were visible enough to these, her two lovers. Perhaps she guessed that one of them, at least, might be near watching for her. That wonderful nightingale began his marvellous song, as if to greet the lonely girl at the window.

Lachlan saw William Eagles' eyes soften, and his grip of the pistol, for pistol it was, loosen. He knew the man with whom he had to deal, and withdrew a few paces behind. William Eagles stood gazing on that young girl, and the gentle presence, together with the glory of the night, and the song of "her melodious bird," stayed the purpose of the half-mad, half-melancholy man. He seemed, after a few minutes had passed, to have forgotten Lachlan's presence. He sat down on the root of a tree, put down the pistol, which Lachlan immediately took possession of, and continued gazing on Aline until she closed the window, and he could see her no longer.

"Now all is dark again," he muttered. "But I have seen her. God bless her—God bless them both, and forgive me! I will leave them to-morrow for ever."

Something like a sob burst from the wretched man. Lachlan's kind heart could not bear this.

"Mr. Eagles," he said, gently, "you are not well enough to bear these night dews. You must come home with me. Then I will tell you why I came here, if you will tell me what brought you here."

William Eagles' strange words had astonished Lachlan, and aroused his suspicions that he must know Aline's mother.

"I—I—I came here—I must not tell," said William Eagles, starting, and endeavouring to rise. He was still very weak. Lachlan helped him up, and drawing his arm within his own, said—

"You must let me see you home; you are not strong yet."

He resisted at first, but finding that he staggered as he moved, he was obliged to yield.

When Lachlan had got him through the brushwood, and into the meadows that led to Yeo, he again said—

"Now I will tell you what brought me to

the Downs Farm, and I must have a similar confidence in return. Perhaps I may be of use to you, if you will be open with me. I went, as you did, to see Aline, but not because I thought she would see me—I knew she would not—but because I love her as well and as purely as ever man loved woman—with a love that brooks no rival—and therefore I will know why *you* were haunting a place that of right belongs to me alone."

"Because she is mine, and only mine. No man has any right to her but me," said William, withdrawing his arm from Lachlan, who let it go readily enough at this declaration.

"That is to say that Aline is false," said Lachlan, "and I do not believe you. She is not yours."

It was now Lachlan's turn to flash fire from his grey eyes into the moonshine.

"Have you made her love you? And do you care for her honour as for her life?" said William Eagles, softening as Lachlan hardened.

"Am I an honest man?" asked Lachlan, fiercely.

"You are a Lyons: proud, obstinate, and— honourable, like your race—and—and unforgiving," said William. "But Aline, nobody knows who she is."

"*I* know," said Lachlan, proudly. "She is good, pure, innocent, and lovely."

"And you would marry her?"

"To-morrow! And work for her, and love her, and for her mother too, as you never could do, William Eagles."

"Then God bless you, Lachlan Lyons! Let me have your arm again; for if she loves you, I too must love you, wretched man that I am."

They walked on a little while in silence. At last William Eagles said, and very solemn and touching was his manner—

"I do not think I have very long to live. You might do me the greatest favour that you ever did to mortal man. I am going to leave Yeo, and to end my days abroad. Perhaps they may be lengthened by the southern climate. But before I go I must see Aline. Do not start. I should have been away weeks ago but that I wanted to have an interview with her first. See her for me. Tell her that it is the one wish of a nearly dying man, and that she may meet me in perfect faith. That I have something to tell her which nearly concerns her and her mother, but which her mother must not know. Tell her that I knew her father, and that it is about him that I would speak. You, yourself, shall settle time and place with her, if you will. You shall even remain within call, and be her protector, if necessary. I am too weak, and have been too ill to care for ways and means, provided only I can see her. If you love her, and pity me, you will do this for both of us. I declare to you that it concerns her as much as me. I did not mean to shoot you, just now—God knows I did not—only to frighten you away from my treasure, my all. I believe you are a good young man, as far as any man can be good, for we are all villains at heart. I have been one, but I am better since my illness, and wish to do right. Will you ask Aline to see me?— Will you try?"

" I will do anything to help her to find her father, or to gain any knowledge of him," said Lachlan.

" Does she care to find him? Has she an interest in him ?"

" I suppose she would have an interest in

him if she has one. At all events, I will tell her what you say, if I can get an opportunity. But I never see her. However, I promise you that I will try, if you solemnly vow to me that you give me your true and only reason for seeking this interview."

"I solemnly vow that I have no other. I would speak to her of her father, and of him alone. You do not know how I love that child, you cannot. I want her not to fear and hate me, as she does. If you will manage this meeting I shall be grateful to you as long as this miserable life lasts. And who knows if you may not help me to a better? Do you believe in a better life? I was an infidel, or tried to be, till I saw Aline, and then I began to believe in heaven, because I felt such a creature could never die."

"Nothing ever dies," said Lachlan. "The pure waters of this little brook live for ever, either in clouds, or dew-drops, or rain, if absorbed, still to live again, and fertilize and bless. And shall the soul, a pure and more subtle essence than this element, ever die? Like these waters, believe me, it will either drag through mud, clay, or some kind of impurity, into stagnation—or worse than stagnation—or be drawn up into sunlight, or ether, to perfect purity."

"Lachlan, you are a poet!" said William Eagles; "a true poet. Is not the true poet the man who finds poetry in all around him? I have had such thoughts in my youth, when I used to gaze upon that gabled window to watch for another Mary. You know Aline's name is Mary, too. Tell me how you—a working man —learnt to be a poet?"

"Whatever poetry is in me was created by my working life," said Lachlan. "All that I turned up out of the earth, blew out of the hard rocks, and saw around and above me, taught me poetry, and Shakspeare was my human master."

"Lachlan, you do me good. Your mind is fresh; and this moonlight softens me. You and Aline might save my soul."

"No; we may pray for you to One who alone can save it. Oh, Mr. Eagles, if you would go to Him, he would by no means cast you out."

Lachlan was too wise to say more. He knew that such a man would brook no preaching, so they made the short remainder of their way in silence until they reached the Nest, where, having first seen Mr. Eagles, Lachlan left him.

CHAPTER V.

WHAT YEO SAID OF KERN.

LACHLAN went almost daily to the Downs during
the ensuing week, but it was not until the following Sunday afternoon that he saw Aline.   All
the inmates of the farm were at church, with
the exception of Aline, her mother, and Mrs.
Bull.   Lachlan was sitting in the hall with
Mrs. Bull, when Aline came down stairs, and
said simply, "Granny, will you go and sit
with mamma, while I talk a little to Lachlan
before he goes away?"

Mrs. Bull was rejoiced to do her bidding,
having a womanly inkling of the state of the
case.

Aline sat down on the settle in the hall,
and Jack, now a very aged daw, hopped out
of his cage to her shoulder.   Lachlan sat

down by her, and Yeo, who was with his master, lay at their feet.

"I have not much time," she said; "but dear mamma could not refuse my request. I am come to say good-bye."

Tears came into Aline's eyes, and her hand found its way into that of Lachlan.

"Not to-day, Aline," said Lachlan. "We must meet once more."

He then told her all that had passed between him and William Eagles. Aline was much agitated.

"Lachlan, what ought I to do?" she said. "I never deceived mamma in my life."

"Could you venture to tell your mamma?"

"No; it would be useless. She would at once forbid our meeting."

"Then I think, for her sake, as well as for your father's sake, you ought to act on your own responsibility."

"If I see him you will be quite near. I am afraid of Mr. William Eagles, though I feel a painful interest .in him. I never cease to think of him."

"Aline!"

Lachlan uttered this one word half reproachfully, and a smile from her sweet, truthful eyes reassured him.

"I feel as if he had some hold on me that I cannot shake off," she said. "His fitful, half-mad ways when I used to see him, convinced me that he knew something of me. I must see him. I feel that it would be right. But where, and how?"

"In *our* dell behind the chapel. Where you first asked me to find your father, and where I may, perhaps, give you news of him through Mr. Eagles. This would not desecrate the place where I found you so unhappy, and where you made me so happy, my Aline."

"It seems very wrong to deceive mamma— to meet him and you secretly—still it must be right to know something of my father, and to try to make dear mamma's mind easy. To-morrow, then, in the nightingale dell. It must be at once, or I shall betray myself."

"I am engaged the whole of to-morrow after ten o'clock," said Lachlan.

"The early morning would be my best time," said Aline, "while mamma is asleep and Fluke busy. I could be there at seven o'clock. I sometimes go out before breakfast to gather a nosegay for mamma. She does not awake till between nine and ten—her nights are so disturbed."

"I will ask William Eagles if he can be up so early. It it can be managed, that we can be in the dell at half-past seven, I will give you a sign."

"A sign? How?"

"If you will look out of your bed-room window at about ten o'clock to-night, I will be by the little bridge over the brook, and wave a white handkerchief."

"How sentimental it all sounds. But it will be quite natural for me to look out at ten o'clock. I knew you went home that way, Lachlan, and sometimes used to see you on the bridge in the moonlight."

Lachlan and Aline put off the thought of parting till the morrow, and talked of other things. Not of love, gentle reader, for Aline had promised her mother that nothing should pass between them but such words as a brother and sister might talk to one another; but not the less, doubtless, was the eternal passion in the heart of each.

But they forgot the time allotted by the mother for the interview, and Mrs. Bull came at last to summon Aline. She was surprised, and somewhat mortified, to see Aline rise at once, shake hands with Lachlan, and run away, without tears or parting words.

" Aline, you have stayed so long !" were the first words of the poor irritable mother, who was lying on a couch by the open window.

"Dear mamma, I see Lachlan so seldom, I forgot the time."

" He is going away soon, I hope."

" I think so ; but the day is not fixed."

" You have bid him good-bye."

" Yes—no—not exactly."

" Then you ought, Aline. At any rate, you cannot see him again."

" He desired to be remembered to you, mamma."

" Thank you. It was a misfortune we ever met him."

" Shall I read the evening service, dear mother ?"

"You have been away so long; there will not be time."

" The Psalms and Lessons, then. It is so

pleasant to read them while the people are at church. One feels as if one were at church too."

"I hope we shall soon be somewhere else, and then you can go to church 'again, Aline. Did Lachlan say nothing amusing?"

"Lachlan said that he was quite in favour with the Miss Daws, and that he had done several things to their property, which had made them once call him nephew."

"Perhaps they will leave him the old manor house, Aline. Then, if he got back the baronetcy, people would forget his being a navvy, and——"

Aline well knew what the "and" meant. Her mother was fond of Lachlan, but she could not part with Aline, or let her marry any one who was not in a certain position.

"I mean," said her mother, "that when I am dead he might marry you if he were better off. What else did he say?"

"That it has been formally announced that Kern is going to be married to Lord Inncaster."

"I thought she would make a grand match. Where is she now?"

"She went up to London yesterday, from Brooklands, where she had been staying three days. She is gone to Dr. Dove's."

"Did Lord Inucaster see her father and relations?"

"Lachlan thinks not. He went to town two days before her."

"Clever girl! What will become of Captain Love?"

"He threatens a breach of promise, and has offended his Aunt Daws very much; so they told Lachlan."

"Why, the old ladies seem to have made a confidant of Lachlan."

"Yes. He was amused by their asking him whether, if he had a chance of recovering any of the family property, he would make a good match?"

"What did he say?"

"That he should be sure to make a good match if he ever married; as he should only marry the girl he loved; and she was very good."

"What nonsense! I suppose he meant you?"

"I think he did, mamma; but he did not tell me so."

"You are both very absurd. Now you may read to me, if you like."

Scarcely had the reading begun, however, when Fluke came in. She was full of the news of Kern's grand match.

"Law! my lady, you never see any one like Mrs. Lyons. She is all wonder, like a hen that has just hatched a young turkey. You should have seen her after church, talking to one and another. She forgot the other little angels, and her sickness, and everythink else in her pride about that 'aughty Kern."

"You will be obliged to call her Lady Inncaster now, Fluke," broke in Aline, maliciously.

"You might be just as grand if you chose, Miss Aline. But to see Mrs. Lyons! Curtseying here: shaking 'ands there: lording it over Mrs. and Miss Love and the doctor. That did me good, that did. Mrs. Love couldn't resist asking if the news was true, and congratulating Mrs. Lyons on the wrong side of her mouth. Says Mrs. Lyons, 'Oh yes, Mrs. Love! it is quite true. My daughter is gone up to my sister's to make preparations.' 'Oh,' says Mrs. Love, 'so soon as all that!

Rather quick, I think. She'll be married from Dr. Dove's, I suppose.' 'Dear no,' says Mrs. Lyons. 'From Lady Nux's. Her ladyship particularly wishes it. Sir John's going abroad soon. Your son's gone away, I believe, ma'am, isn't he.' This was as much as to say that Kern had refused 'em both; and the report is that she 'as: the proud minx!"

Madam Rambully laughed a laugh of satisfaction.

"What did the Miss Daws do?" asked Aline.

"Oh! they bowed their big poke bonnets to Mrs. Lyons as grand as ever, and only the youngest stopped for a minute by the sly, just to ask Kezia if it was really true that her sister was going to marry an earl. Poor Kezia, who is frightened to death at it all, said she believed so, and turned away, looking as unappy as if Kern had run away with a tinker. The churchyard was as full, after church, as if there was a funeral. I kept close to Mrs. Lyons all the time, and heard everything. As for the boys and Rhoda, they were swelling out like young goslings."

"And Mr. Lyons?" asked Aline.

"He walked 'ome as faust as he could through the little gate; but I could see he looked as proud as a peacock. He does look a gentleman, as I always say. There is something in good blood, though you don't care to think so, Miss Aline."

"Oh yes I do, Fluke. I always thought all the Lyons' family gentlefolks. But so I think daddy and granny, who don't pretend to family. Do they know about Kern? I must just run and ask granny."

"Let me finish first, Miss Aline. They say that Captain Love has gone off to London after Kern, and that Sir John is going away soon. *You* might have ad Sir John, Miss Aline. I know he used to admire you most, and was always 'ankering about this 'ouse."

"But it isn't too late yet, Fluke."

"Well! you was born without proper pride. Lachlan would be better than Kern's cast-offs."

"I think, Fluke, you may say *Mr.* to him, at least," said Madam Rambully. "Now you may get my tea. Aline, ask Mrs. Bull to come here if she is disengaged. I think I could see Mr. Bull, too, this afternoon. He amuses me."

Aline soon brought Mr. and Mrs. Bull to her mother, who heard from them all that she wanted to hear about Kern.

"Farmer Bull of the Downs, with an earl for a grandson," said that worthy. "Granny has been quite beside herself ever since we heard it. We didn't believe John yesterday. We're going to give up farming directly, and go to Lunnen, all of us. Kern would like to see us at her wedding. The wench always said she'd marry a gentleman, and much good may 't do her. Job and Rhoda and the children went to Brooklands to see her, as my lady was too high to go home, I suppose. Some sort of message came to us, old folk; but we weren't going to dance after a brat like that. I'd rather she'd married John Dull for my peart."

"She'll make a very good countess, Mr. Bull," said Madam Rambully. "She was born for it. Lord Inncaster is a very good man."

"Do you know him, madam?"

"I have heard of him."

"She's lost to us for ever," sobbed Mrs. Bull. "How can she ever get to heaven with all that pride and grandeur?"

"She wouldn't know her relations there, any how, grammer," said Mr. Bull. "As to our daughter Rhoda, she hops about like a hen on a hot gridiron, and don't know whether she stands on her head or her heels. And I'll warrant daughter Dove 'll be just the same. Women are never content in the station in which they were born. Rhoda thought it grand to marry Job; and now! there'll be no stopping her tongue."

"But Kern went away in very bad spirits," said Mrs. Bull. "I'm afraid she'll not be happy with all her grandeur. How should she, and marrying a man as old as her father? An old lord's no better than an old farmer, as I see. Spring and winter never did agree, and never will. Granfer and I are within a few years of one another, and I hope we shall die as we've lived, close together. There oughtn't to be a great disparity between husband and wife. Poor Kern! She had her good parts, too. "Mrs. Oliver Bat went to see her before she left; I took that very kind. Now I thought she'd have been set up by her marriage, but she's humbler than before. She's always asking for you, madam, and for missey. The poor old gentleman, her father, is nearly worn out by waiting on his son. I don't think either of 'em is long for this world." .

Madam Rambully and Aline both started, and the former, turning very pale, said that her leg suddenly gave her great pain, and she was afraid that she must call Fluke.

The little party was at once broken up, and Madam Rambully left with Aline and Fluke.

Aline had some difficulty in keeping her mother amused that evening. Each was pre-occupied. Aline was thinking of the interview in prospect, and her mother could talk of nothing but of leaving the Downs. Every now and then she was seized with a feverish anxiety to change her abode, and nothing but her leg, which was not yet well, kept her at the farm.

CHAPTER VI.

ALINE FINDS HER FATHER.

THE following morning Aline, Lachlan, and William Eagles were in the nightingale dell at half-past seven o'clock. Aline arrived a few minutes before the others, and stood trembling like the one first autumn leaf that quivered on the tree above her head. The dew lay thick on the grass, the air was chill, and the morning mists of a September day had scarcely cleared off. She felt that she was taking a decided step on her own responsibility, and like an unfledged bird that first leaves the nest alone, she looked round her with some terror. But the recollection of her former meeting with Lachlan in that dell, and the promise he then made her to help her to find her father gave her courage.

It was to his side that she went, as for protection, when he and William Eagles entered the dell, and his firm glance reassured her.

As she shook hands with William, pity soon took the place of fear. He was so much altered by illness that she would scarcely have known him. Her first natural words put them all at their ease.

"I am very sorry that you have been so ill. Do sit down on this root, and then you can tell me what you know of my father."

Lachlan said that Mr. William Eagles wished him to hear the conversation if Aline had no objection. She gladly assented, and then William Eagles spoke for the first time: some strong emotion had prevented his even greeting Aline.

"Will you sit down by me?" he said. "I could better collect my thoughts if you were by my side."

The large roots of a tree on which Aline had spent many a happy, dreamy hour, afforded seats for both, and Aline sat down almost at his feet. Lachlan leant against the tree on the other side, and stood gazing at the pair, and wondering what there was in the eyes of each as they looked at one another, that was so much alike. At that moment William's eyes were softened, and Aline's kindled by some great inward feeling.

"You have heard your mother's history, as she would tell it you, and consequently all she knows of your father's," he began.

"All, I believe," said Aline.

"And knowing this, you would still wish to hear further of your father?"

"I would."

"You do not hate your father?"

"Oh no! I would give my life to see him united once more to my mother."

William Eagles started, and put his hand on Aline's head.

"God bless you!" he said.

She withdrew in affright, and he restrained himself.

"Forgive me. Your father was and is my most intimate friend, and I rejoiced for him."

"My father is still alive, then?"

"He is."

"Tell me where—tell me quickly all you know of him. I will go all over the world to bring him to my mother."

William Eagles put his hands before his eyes, and when he removed them, Aline saw that they had wiped away tears. That little hand of hers that could not resist soothing sorrow, was laid on the large, thin, white hands, and instantly clasped within them.

" Leave it here, child; leave it here. Even Lachlan could not object to your father's bosom-friend holding it a little while. I may never hold it again."

And so the hand remained.

"If you know all your mother's story, I have not much to tell, and what I would say, is more to make you pity your father, than to extenuate his conduct. When he first saw your mother, he was engaged to be married to another woman, whom he dearly loved. She was beautiful as the day, and pure as an angel, but without either fortune or education. Your mother had both, and was elegant and accomplished as well. When your father first saw her he was much taken with her, and as you know, the liking was mutual.

" By degrees he forgot, or tried to forget his first love, in the greater worldly advantages promised to him by his second.

"No one knows better than I do, the temptations of art. To improve oneself in this divine gift of painting, and to visit the land where pictures and painters are the finest, is to be happy. So we artists think in our youth. So thought your father.

" He married your mother then, for the two-fold reason that he greatly admired her, and that her fortune would enable him to pursue his insane passion for art. He did not care for her fortune for any other reason, although he probably would not have deserted his first and purest love, had she not possessed one.

"Doubtless your mother gave you the history of their marriage, and subsequent disagreement. He was passionate, self-willed, fond of society, gay, extravagant,—reckless indeed in money matters; she was proud, reserved, irritable, and, in every respect, unsuited to him. If his faults were grave, she made them graver by her repelling reserve, even when he was penitent.

"But I do not wish to justify his conduct, which was unjustifiable; still, I must say, that he would never have been so violent, had she been less provoking.

"The estrangement was gradual, and her resolute refusal to let him have the money he required to pursue his search in the kingdom of art, completed it. In this she was wrong. Money is only useful, inasmuch as it ministers to the higher aims of mankind.

" I will not pain you by going through the differences of your parents. Your father was passionate, your mother reserved, and the general end of each quarrel was utter silence on the part of the latter, and consequent alienation of affection on that of the former. Your mother was said to have cried herself blind,—I—your father I mean,—never saw her weep. Such was her pride and obstinacy, that she would submit even to blows as stoically as a Spartan woman.

" At last, I suppose, they ended by hating one another.

" Meanwhile you were kept out of your father's sight. Children were disagreeable to him, and he only saw in you the offspring of a tiresome, proud woman, who came in the way of his advancement. Heavens! how he would adore you now!

" Under all these aggravating circumstances,

he considered himself justified in leaving your mother to herself.

"I suppose you know her real name and your own—Aquile; I may as well call her so. Signora d'Aquile was, doubtless, happier without him, as he was without her: at least he then thought so.

"He fell in love with a hundred beautiful Italians. You start! I dare say you think Lachlan could never love any one but you— he is ready to swear it. Be it so. All men are not so constant, and all women are not Alines. However, there was one woman, and she was of noble birth, and good fortune, whom he admired above all the rest. He made up his mind to marry her. Signora d'Aquile had frequently given him to understand that she wished to see him no more, and he had made people believe her dead.

"She was at Venice. He had been absent from her for a long time, but before taking the final step of deserting her, and making another woman his wife, he wished to see her, and to discover whether she really hated him. He also wanted some money—not exactly for his marriage, but to pay debts, contracted in his capacity of artist. He believes that had she then received him kindly, he should have given up this marriage, as he was not wholly wicked, though bad enough, as the world counts badness.

"He was touched by finding her ill, and very weak. Her blindness was increasing, and there was a sort of mournful dignity in her appearance, which excited his remorse and compassion, at first sight. They were apparently friends for a day or two, and he was almost impelled to abandon his intention of leaving her; to pay his debts, and to become a better man. But he asked her for money, and then the real nature of the woman burst forth. She stood up before him, and braved him. She told him of his extravagance, desertion, libertinage, want of fatherly love, deceit, heartlessness; and finally flung in his teeth that she knew he was married to another. She told him that all she wished, was never to see him again. That he might live for ever with this, his mistress, and never fear her troubling him with her presence. He was to go his way, and she would go hers. Pride would prevent her interfering with his pleasures—blindness her ever seeing him again.

"I cannot—your father could not—describe the cold, haughty, sarcastic manner, and the biting, hard, irritating words in which she allowed her anger to explode. All he could tell was, that as they culminated in withering scorn and hate, so his wrath reached its height. He was never master of himself in his maddening passion; and it was, as a madman, that he rushed upon her, and knocked her down, vowing, as he did so, that she should have her will, and that he would never see her again.

"He left the house instantly, and did not return for some time.

"He went on a sketching tour for about a month, and had time for reflection, and some self-reproach. When he returned to Venice, he was impelled to go once more to inquire if the Signora d'Aquile was still there. The padrona told him that she was dead and buried, and that as he was undoubtedly her murderer, he had better take himself away, as the officers of justice were looking after him, and came to her house every other day in search of him.

" He was stunned by this intelligence. As if by magic, all the first love that he had felt for his wife, returned, and with it the remorse of a Cain. The woman saw his agony, and seemed for a moment to pity him ; but the next accused him of the murder, and said he deserved to be miserable for life. He asked her where his child was, and she said she supposed she was at school, but she did not know : adding, hastily, that he had better go away, as she expected the police every minute.

" Beside himself, he obeyed her command, mechanically ; but returned again and again, in spite of his danger. All that he could ascertain from the padrona was, that the blow he had given your mother, had killed her on the spot—that the police had been called in— that they were in search of him—that they had buried her in a churchyard not far distant —and that everything belonging to her had been sold to defray the expenses of the funeral. This information your father obtained with difficulty, and amid threats of delivering him up to justice.

" He found his way into the signora's old

apartments, but saw nothing there belonging to her, except the stain of half-washed out blood on the carpet, in the place where she had stood when he had knocked her down.

" At this sight he wanted no more incentives to flight, but left the house and its mistress for ever. Before the day was over, he had visited the grave that he believed, from the landlady's description, to be that of his wife, and fled from Venice. He wrote an account of all these circumstances to the lady for whom he had forsaken his wife, and never saw her again.

" He went to the school at which he was given to understand you had last been placed by your mother, and learnt that you had been fetched from thence by an Italian servant, upon plea of your mother's being very ill, and had never returned. The mistress of the school told him that she had received a cheque for the amount due for your tuition, but she did not know from whom ; she also spoke to your unhappy father of your loving nature, of your affection for your companions and of theirs for you, and of your docility and aptitude in learning. It was then, for the first time, that he longed for your love, and lamented over all that he had cast away from him.

"But he was to bear the full penalty of all his crimes. You weep, my child—my—my Aline. God bless you for your tears! Many a weary day and night has your wretched father wept, but never washed away the stains of his heart.

" For nearly ten years he wandered about in search of you. During the whole of this time he painted for bread enough to sustain life,—and that was all. Still he became famous. His name is known all over Europe as that of a great artist. But what does he care for fame? Murder is at the bottom of it. A dead wife and a deserted child are ever before his eyes, haunting him while he paints, reproaching him when the world praises, convicting him when he seems the most honoured.

"He came to England, and visited, in disguise, the neighbourhood where your mother once lived, but all that he could learn of her was, that she was reported to be dead, and no one knew anything of her child.

"This, Aline, is your father's history—as much of it, at least, as it concerns you to

know. Other sins he has committed, and
heavy ones, against parent, sister—but I am
forgetting myself.   He is, at this present time,
a miserable, lonely man.   He feels that God's
curse is upon him, if, indeed, there be a God.
He is ill—dying, perhaps.   Aline, Aline, shall
I tell him that you forgive him, that you will
try not to hate him?   Speak, my darling, do
not sob so piteously.   Say but one word of
comfort for your unhappy father."

Here William Eagles ceased speaking.
Aline was sobbing violently, her head resting
on her lap, her hand still firmly grasped by
William.   Lachlan was gazing on the pair,
an expression of anxious uncertainty in his
face.   He was the first to speak after a brief
silence.

"Aline! look up, Aline."

Aline looked up, and rose as she did so.
She stood beside Lachlan, sobbing still, as if
unable to speak.

"Dear Aline," continued Lachlan; "you
asked me to find you your father.   I am sure
that I have done so.   He is before you.   Mr.
Eagles has been telling his own tale.   It is
useless and wrong to torture you with suspense,

and you are too good to be alarmed by any sudden disclosure. May God help you to comfort your father!"

"Is it true? say, is it true?" cried Aline, turning her bewildered eyes from Lachlan to William.

William Eagles got up hastily, saying—

"True—too true; my child, my angel! Only say, 'I do not hate you,' call me 'father' once, and I——"

Before the sentence was finished, Aline was in his arms.

"Father! father!" was all she could say, as she nearly fainted in those arms that encircled her, and pressed her in an embrace such as she had never felt before.

"My darling—my child! Have I killed you?" cried the newly found father.

"No—no!" sobbed Aline. "Thank God for all—for all. I do not hate you—I will love you, I will give you back again to mamma. But I do not believe it yet. Tell me, Lachlan, is it true?"

Againsh e went to Lachlan, as if for protection and assurance.

"It must be true, Aline."

"Then I will go to mamma, and tell her and ask her——"

"No—no—she will never forgive me. All I ask is your forgiveness, my child, and then I will leave you both in peace for ever."

"She must forgive you. You must love one another again. We must be happy. I do not understand it, but if you are really my father, promise me not to go away. I cannot believe it. Mr. Eagles my grandfather—Ellen my aunt—you—you—my father?"

"It grieves you, Aline, and I do not wonder."

"No—I am thankful. But it is very strange. How can I be sure, Lachlan? Quite sure?"

"Aline, did not your mother run away in terror at the sound of my voice, and break her leg in doing so?" said William Eagles. "And can you not remember that I nearly died in her room, when I placed her on her bed, and found out who she was?"

"I do—I do!" cried Aline, and again flung her arms round his neck.

William Eagles shed the first tears he had shed for many a year, and almost for the first time in his life, uttered those solemn words so often thoughtlessly said, "God bless you, my child!"

Lachlan walked to a little distance to let the tears that had gathered in his eyes fall, and to leave the father and child alone for a little space.

The morning sunbeams pierced through the trees, the birds sang, the brook murmured, and the turf and flowers shone in the quivering light. Lachlan breathed a silent prayer to heaven for her whom he loved, and for the father she had found. He forgot himself and his hopes in them and theirs.

"Lachlan!" called Aline, "I must go to mamma. Take care of my father—my father! I am so bewildered, that I scarcely know what to do or say. But do not let him go away."

"I will not go until you tell me, my darling," said William. "I will grow well and good for your sake. I feel better already. I will obey you in everything."

"Then go home now, and I will see what I can say to mamma, and tell Lachlan to-morrow. You will come to the Downs to-morrow, Lachlan?"

"Yes," said Lachlan, not daring to say that it would be the last time.

Lachlan held one of Aline's trembling hands, her father the other.

"God bless you both!" said William; "and forgive me. I am not yet deserving of the name of father—when I am, may you both call me so."

A glorious sunbeam broke through the trees upon the little group, as if to hallow those words of penitence, and one of Aline's larks, high, high in air, took them up in its song, and carried them away to the gates of heaven.

CHAPTER VII.

ALINE RESISTS HER MOTHER.

ALINE went to her own room, and knelt down to pray to the Almighty to give her strength for the task she had resolved to accomplish at once. She believed that in matters of right and wrong, life and death, no time was to be lost; so she asked her Heavenly Father to help her to save her earthly one, and to reconcile her mother to him. She was, as she had said, bewildered, still she saw her duty very plainly, and resolved to do it.

She evaded Fluke's rigorous questioning, and went to her mother as soon as she was ready to see her, begging Fluke not to interrupt them.

Madam Rambully (we must continue to call her by this name) was lying on a couch near the window, as usual, in her white morning-gown.

"You are late to-day, Aline. Where have you been?" she said, as Aline entered.

"I have been in the nightingale bower, dearest mother."

Aline's voice trembled.

"There is something the matter with you, child. What have you been doing there?"

"Dear mother, if I tell you what I have been doing, you must try neither to be angry with me, nor to excite yourself."

She took her mother's hand.

"Your hand is like ice, Aline. You tremble all over. I feel that you are pale as death. What is the matter?"

Aline knelt down by her mother's side, laid her head on her lap and sobbed uncontrollably.

"Mother, dear mother, be patient with me, be tender of yourself. I—I know that I have a living father."

Madam Rambully started, but, as if half prepared for the announcement, said sternly—

"Who dared to tell you that, Aline?"

Aline had expected an outburst of passionate grief, the calmness re-assured her.

"Oh, mother, the promptings of nature have almost told it me often, but to-day I have found it out myself. Have pity on him—have pity on him!"

"On whom?"

"On my poor, unhappy father."

"When I told you the story of my life and wrongs, you promised me never to name him again, Aline. You will at once be silent."

"I cannot, mamma. I must break my promise, and disobey you. Having found my father, I have a divided duty to perform, and you must at least hear what I have to say."

"Aline, if you wish to kill me at once, go on."

"Dear mamma, you know how I love you. I only wish to secure your peace of mind, and I can secure it, even now, if you will only let me."

"Peace of mind! Do not mock me with the words. That can only be insured by leaving this place at once, and seeking another whither *he* cannot come."

"The hand of God is stronger than your will, dear mother. As it has brought you into this place, where my father and all his relations live——"

"Aline, if you call that man father, you shall leave me for ever, and go to him."

"Oh, mamma; be pitiful. Your wrongs have been truly great, but not so great as you believe. And we are commanded to forgive even our bitterest enemies."

"Not when they are formed out of our nearest friends."

"Were not those 'wounds which I received in the house of my friends,' the example for us, dear mother ?"

"Aline, you argue in vain, I recognized the voice I hated when I stumbled and broke my leg. I have been expecting something of this kind ever since, and that is why I have been so anxious to get away. Why am I never to have peace ?"

"You never can until you are reconciled to him, and he can never find it, until you have forgiven him. He has been a wanderer all over the world, alone and wretched, and haunted by remorse, ever since he last saw you."

"And knocked me down ! ha ! ha ! He was

too wholly a brute to care for knocking me down."

"Signora Bettini told him that he had murdered you—even showed him where you were buried, and——"

"Admirable woman! That accounts for my having been so long unmolested. Aline, this is new and amusing; you may tell me more."

"He has been suffering torments ever since."

"I am charmed to hear it. He deserves to suffer, not only on my account, I find, but on that of others. Since you are determined to annoy me, we may as well recapitulate. You see, knowing the voice, unfortunately but too well,—it was melodious enough when it chose— I have been making inquiries. I find that this 'voice' belonged to the man who having first made me blind and lame, picked me up, and brought me into this room. The name, they tell me, is William Eagles, which my knowledge of Italian soon enables me to turn into *Aquile*. This noble man—painter, sculptor, poet, and what not—originated from the 'Nest.' A poetical idea, I presume of the parent Eagle, who brought up a fine pair of young ones in it.

For myself I suddenly find that I am in a hornet's and not an eagle's nest, since I am dropped, heaven knows how, into the very midst of them all.   My venerable father-in-law, my amiable sister-in-law, are close at hand, and I am actually living under the same roof with the parents of my dead and injured rival. Aline, will you dare to name this man again to me ?"

"Mamma, I must.   He is ill and broken-hearted."

"Then he knows what he has made me and Mary Bull suffer."

"He only asks for your forgiveness."

"That he will never have."

"Oh ! mamma; how cruel.   If you only saw him."

"Happily he has prevented my enjoying that pleasure, by depriving me of sight."

"Darling mother, I did not mean to remind you of that.   He says he loved you—but——"

"But, there were Mary Bull, and Signora this, and Signorina that, whom he loved better. I wish to drop the subject, Aline."

"But having found that he lives, known him, even loved him so long, although not as—

although only as Mr. Eagles' son—*I* can never drop it, mamma."

"How dared he make himself known to you?"

"To ask me not to hate him."

"How could you do anything but hate him? He never cared for you, scarcely ever saw you, when he might have won your love."

"Still, dear mamma, I have always prayed for him, and loved him, as——Ever since you told me your story, I have prayed for him, and resolved to find him, and give him back to you. And God has helped me in a way I little thought of. If you could only see his hand in bringing you here—in leading you both to the chapel, when the preacher ——"

"Do not mention the fanatic. His words have haunted me ever since."

"They were true words; you believe the Bible, and you know they must be true."

"I wish you did not preach so, Aline. I hate a preaching woman; Kern never preached. When is she to be married?"

"I do not know. Kern is very clever, but she never would have loved you as I love you, even if she had been your daughter. Why does not your heart leap, as mine did, when you hear that you may make my——your—— a human being happy? I could give up all my own prospects of happiness to insure his."

"Even with Lachlan?"

"Yes; I could resign myself never to see him again, if I could only unite you once more to him you must still love."

"You are a strange girl, Aline. You cannot love Lachlan if you would not give up father and mother for his sake."

"Yes, mamma: I love him very dearly. I shall never love any one else in the same way. But I am not his yet—I am yours, and my father's; and I mean to devote myself, with God's help, to you both, until you no longer need me."

"I shall need you as long as I live, Aline. You will not give me up, I suppose, for this newly-found tie?"

"Oh, mother, why will you not see that the knot is indissoluble that binds you together, and me to both in one. If you cut it, I never can. You will always be joined in my eyes."

"And you can talk calmly of giving up Lachlan?"

"I shall never give him up. He will be the same to me absent or present, for I love him. If I were to go away from Yeo to-morrow, I should never give up my friends here.   I love Mrs. Bat, and think of her just as much as ever, although I have not spoken to her since her return, because you forbade me.   Mother, real love, once conceived in a true heart, never dies."

"Don't cry, Aline ; I did not mean to pain you.   I love you, at least, with all my poor worthless heart.   Tell me what that man said in extenuation of his conduct."

"Nothing, mamma.   He blamed himself entirely.   All that he said was, that he might not have been quite so bad, had you been less reserved, proud, and cold."

"Really ! and then ?"

"That his passion overcame his reason, so that he became almost a madman."

"Quite, I should say.   But what of the woman he was going to marry ?"

"He never saw her after he believed that he had murdered you."

"What is he like ?"

"A wild, pale, attenuated ghost."

"I am no believer in ghosts. You think he is really ill?"

"The doctors thought him dying a little while ago."

"I know all that. But now?"

"They say he is in a decline; but I believe he might yet live, if you would let him see you, and would forgive him. Oh darling mother, one word, only one word."

Aline fell on her knees by her mother's side, and clasped both her hands in hers.

"I implore you as a wife, a mother, a Christian woman—*my* mother, my darling mother— have pity on him, on me!"

Madam Rambully suppressed, with a great effort, some inward emotion.

"Aline, you excite me too much; were I to forgive him to-morrow, he would cause me the same misery the next day, and the next."

"No, no, dearest mother. He is as gentle as a lamb when kindness is shown him. I should be near to love you both—to draw you together—oh, he loves me so, it breaks my heart to think of his going away from me. Think of me—his child, your child—ready to give myself up to you, and live for you both.

Have mercy on me, if not on him, and on yourself. Oh, Heavenly Father, soften my mother's
heart, for I cannot!"

Aline laid her head on her mother's lap, and
sobbed aloud. Tears fell from that mother's
eyes upon the prostrate child.

There was a long silence, during which Aline
prayed earnestly.

"Aline," at last said her mother, "I cannot
pursue this subject to-day. I will think of it
—dream upon it—try to pray upon it, as you
would wish me, and see if my feelings change.
I must acknowledge to you, and so please your
loving heart, that what you have said has
affected me.   A broken-spirited, repentant
man, if he is really willing to leave me in
peace, may, in time, obtain forgiveness, but
nothing more. At present I can only feel
angry that he has discovered himself to you;
though, seeing you, one can scarcely wonder.
Leave me for a short time, and when I am
calm, I will see you again."

Aline threw her arms round her mother's
neck, kissed her, and went again to her own
room to think and pray.

Madam Rambully, left to herself, unlocked

a case, which she always kept near her, and took from it a miniature of her husband. It was remarkably handsome. She put it close to her eyes, as if she would endeavour to decypher the features. Her sight had slightly improved, since her mind had been diverted from it to her leg. She thought as follows :—

" This face changed to attenuation and suffering! The man I loved so madly, ill and penitent! All this long struggle against my love once more ended by his presence, and my child a petitioner for my forgiveness! Is it, as she said, Providence, or is it fate and chance, that bring us together in spite of ourselves? I would have fled from him at the first sound of his voice, but I was chained by this broken leg. My faint hope that he did not recognize me, is destroyed by his discovering himself to Aline. And my heart, which I fancied adamant, beat as wildly as ever, when she said that he had never seen that woman since, and loved me still. I try not to believe it, and I dare not see him, for one word from him would conquer me—but God knows I forgive him. I have forgiven him, ever since I knew of his dreadful illness. And He knows too, how

I have wearied Fluke with questions about him, and been careless of myself so that he might recover. Is Aline right, and is love stronger than death; or, what is more to the point, stronger than cruelty and dishonour? I am so weak—so very weak. My God, whom I have so long forgotten, deign to help thine erring, suffering child! 'Proud, cold, and reserved,' I have been, I know—hardened and impenitent. Thou hast tried me with every earthly ill, but I have not yielded. Ten years of hardness of heart against Thee, and him whom I called husband. Was it the prayer of my child that suddenly broke the chain, and loosened the icy barrier? If so, hear me also, even me, oh! my Father."

Madam Rambully covered her face with her hands, and prayed. When had she so prayed before? Was it her child's prayer that had induced hers? And had their gracious Master in heaven softened the mother's heart for the innocent child's sake? Who shall say? That heart had been so long callous through previous suffering, that nothing but the dew of heavenly grace could find its way there. And it may be that the dew had fallen.

But Madam Rambully did not speak on the subject to Aline again that day. Fluke was indignant with Aline for exciting her mamma, until she saw that something had passed between them that was not to be confided to her, and then she was indignant on her own account.

The day wore through, and the following morning brought Lachlan, before Aline had had any further conversation with her mother. She told her, however, that she must see Lachlan once more, and receiving an assent—apparently a careless one, as if from a pre-occupied mind —she went to him.

She told him of the conversation that she had had with her mother about her father, and begged him to see the latter, and to tell him to be patient and hope, as she believed her mother was softening towards him.

" I shall succeed in reconciling them, if life is lengthened for us all," she said ; " I feel sure that I shall."

When Lachlan had heard all that Aline could say about her parents, he asked her if she would walk a little way with him, as he was obliged to leave at once. She consented, and while putting on her bonnet, he went to look for Mr. and Mrs. Bull, in order to wish them a hasty good bye. Having done so, he and Aline took their way across the fields.

After a brief silence, he told Aline that it was for her to settle whether he should accept the Russian engagement or not.

" For me ?" said Aline.

" Yes," answered Lachlan. " If you could give me any hope that I might ask you to be my wife, I would relinquish it at once, that I might find work in England, and be near your parents."

" Lachlan, I can give *you* no hope, for I have none myself. At present, and for an indefinite period, my duty is with my parents. When I have brought them together, as I must and shall, I must keep them together. I must live with them, nurse them, accommodate their discordant minds, as only a daughter could do; devote my whole time to them in short. I must still be eyes to mamma, and clearer ones than I have hitherto been; and strength and comfort to my father, and——"

" And nothing to me, who love you better than they love you ?"

" Yes—your true and constant friend : your sister : your——"

"Everything but my wife, Aline. You do not know how I love you—how I would love your parents, and bear with them for your sake."

"No, Lachlan, that cannot be. I shall never change, and we are both young: let us hope. But you must follow your profession, and become famous for my sake. It would be my pride to hear of you as a great man. An engineer hero—for there are such, just as much as soldier heroes,—and going on doing good, as you havedo ne hitherto. You would write to my father, and he would write to you, and perhaps, in time, I might be allowed to write to you. And when we are all three happy together,—which we shall be soon, I know— your letters will be our pleasure and pride. Papa likes you — what a pretty sound the word has ! — and mamma really likes you, and I—I care for you a very little, you know; and we shall look forward to your delightful letters as to a festival. And you will think of me as very happy with everybody I love best become my real living relations ; and reigning at the Nest, and the Lodge, and somewhere else, with the parents. Oh, Lachlan, I feel like the girl going to market, with her basket of eggs—only mine will not fall down and break as hers did."

Aline's wish to cheer Lachlan brought back her own hopeful spirit; and as she painted her imaginary future, she fully believed that it would come to pass, and looked at Lachlan with the old happy, trustful face, that he knew and loved so well. He did not dare to cast the shadow of a doubt over the bright path she fancied she was walking in, so answered her as cheerfully as he could :

"I may be away some years—it is impossible to say how long—and I may not make either money or fame. Would you love me still, Aline ?"

"Just as well, perhaps better; for you always will be Lachlan the loyal, as Kern once christened you. But I know you will do some great work, and the Emperor will reward you, and when you come back to Yeo, the bells will ring, and the band will play, and it will be far grander than as if you really got back the title. Can't you fancy old Dick Crow breaking the last string of his fiddle, and little Johnny Setter cracking his cheeks with blowing the clarionet ?"

"That must be when we are married, Aline."

" So it shall—and daddy shall play ' Haste to the wedding,' on his bass viol."

The pair laughed heartily, and just as their sudden mirth rang through the trees under which they were walking, William Eagles came upon them.

" So merry, my children, already? Then there must be good news?" he said, taking Aline's hand, and kissing her.

" I have settled it all," she said. " You must have patience a little longer, and I am sure all will be right. Mamma is much calmer than I expected. She was not angry with me, and asked about you with more of interest than annoyance. I know she would love you again, if she were quite sure you love her. She thinks you feel remorse, not love, and will not open her whole heart until she sees into yours."

" Tell her—swear to her for me—that when I saw her lying on that bed—pale, lifeless, as I thought—twice murdered, I believed—I suddenly felt the passion of such love revive in my heart as I never felt but once before—lover, husband, all in one. But in that house, where they hate me so, it was succeeded by a horror of remorse so deadly, that when the old man cursed me, and when I thought I saw Mary Bull's ghost, and when I fell down as dead, and was dragged home by Lachlan, I grew mad. Love, hate, revenge, remorse, grief, pain— Pandora's box without the Hope at the bottom —fell upon me, and I cared for nothing but death. I should have destroyed myself but for you. I would have you call me 'Father' before I died. Since yesterday I have changed. That blessed word 'Father, father—*my* father,' has rung in my ears to the tune of Mendelssohn's 'Wedding March.' I have been singing it so loud that my own poor old father came to answer to the call. And then I made him happy by telling him that I was changed, and better. Ellen, too, told me that I was looking like my true old self, and kissed me twenty times in her joy. My child, my Aline! this is your doing; finish it, and may the blessing of your heavenly Father repay you for the blessing you will have been to your earthly one!"

The ready tears were beginning to chase the smiles from Aline's sweet eyes as her father spoke.

" Lachlan, comfort him ; for I must go away," she said.

Lachlan's cheeks flushed.

" May I see you for five minutes before I leave to-morrow?" he said. " I can then take one last message to your father for you. And I may, perhaps, quit England with the consciousness of his probable re-union with your mother."

Aline thought for a moment, then said—

" If you will come to the farm, and if mamma will let me, I will see you once more. So we will not say good-bye, Lachlan, that word of many sorrows."

Again a hand in the hands of her friends, and Aline was gone, begging Lachlan, as she hastened away, to walk home with her father.

CHAPTER VIII.

LACHLAN CHANGES HIS MIND.

WILLIAM EAGLES was going to the Downs Lodge, and Lachlan went with him. They found Mrs. Oliver in the library with her husband. She was working, and he was reading aloud to her. They both rose as they saw their friends pass the window, and went out to meet them.

"I *am* so glad to see you," said Ellen, kissing her brother then and there.

"I can't say that I am," growled Oliver. "This is the very first visit you have paid us, William, since we came home."

"This is the first time that I have been strong enough to walk so far," was the answer. "Ellen, I never saw you look so well and handsome before."

"Then come and take her picture. My

brothers want it done, with Aline, the white greyhound at her feet."

"Aline!" exclaimed William and Lachlan together.

"When did you see the true Aline?" asked Ellen. "I cannot think what is the matter with her. I have sought her, followed her, written to her even; but she avoids me so resolutely that I have not spoken to her since my return. I feel sure it is her mother's fault. But I wish you would tell her, Lachlan, if you see her, how much she distresses me. I had hoped she would have come to see us constantly, and I am sadly disappointed."

"If I see her again I will deliver your message," said Lachlan; "but I am going away to-morrow."

Lachlan then said that he was come to say good-bye, and told them of his prospects.

"You had better not leave the *verd antiques* down at Yeo," said Mr. Oliver. "You are in high favour just now, and have good chance of the heirship."

"I cannot give up my profession for a chance," said Lachlan.

"They say that Bob Love has sold out

of the army, and is gone nobody knows where," said Ellen. "He was sincerely attached to Kern, and she has been his ruin."

"Finished it, you should say, my dear," said Mr. Oliver.

"She was utterly heartless," said Ellen.

"I do not think so," stammered Lachlan.

"What! Not heartless? When I saw her the day before she left for London, she told me, with the self-possession of a cynic philosopher —of Oliver himself—that she chose to marry Lord Inncaster because he suited her. He was a gentleman, and she believed she was a lady, and that was all that was really necessary to make the married state comfortable: inasmuch as true gentlefolks would not do anything rude or disagreeable to one another. I said that she looked ill, which she did; and she told me that it was only from having had an *embarras de richesses* in the matter of beaux. I could make nothing of her, so I wished her joy, and left her."

Here Mr. Bat and Mr. Nicholas came in. They were always very kind to Lachlan, and asked him to dinner at once. He declined, but William consented to remain.

"Ellen gives us first-rate dinners," said Mr. Bat. "She is the best housekeeper I ever saw. Only fancy a woman who has written a novel being a good housekeeper!"

"I couldn't have believed it," said Nicholas. Oliver shrugged his shoulders.

"She is utterly spoilt between you old bachelors. Why do you make me so jealous?"

"Ha! ha! Nol. You're a rum fish—a rum fish."

When Lachlan had wished them all good-bye, and was walking alone and melancholy over the downs, Mr. Nicholas came puffing after him. He was more corpulent than ever, and Oliver said that Ellen would have to answer for it.

"I say, Lachlan," he began, "you remember your poor mother. For her sake, take this from her old friend."

Mr. Nicholas thrust something into Lachlan's hand, and turned hastily homewards. It was a cheque for fifty pounds. Lachlan was about to follow him, and thank him.

"No—no! I cannot bear it," said poor Nicholas. "Not a word, if you would keep my friendship. For her sake!—for her sake!"

Much affected, and very grateful, Lachlan walked on, until he came to the Manor, where he was staying for a few days. There he found a letter from Mr. Markman, telling him that he would not be wanted in London for a week. This seemed like a reprieve. Then he went to call on the Misses Daw, according to the royal commands of those ladies. They received him most graciously. In a short time Miss Margery said—

"Why need you go so far away? Would it not be possible for you to remain in this, the place of your mother's nativity?"

"Yes; of your mother's nativity?" echoed Miss Ann.

"Oh, do, my dear!" sighed Miss Harriet.

"I should not make bread and cheese, much less fame and fortune," said Lachlan.

"I admire your sentiments; they are praiseworthy," said Miss Daw. "But could you not undertake to superintend our property, and to turn to advantage the minerals you say it contains? We would give you a hundred a year!"

"A hundred a year!" said Miss Ann, lifting up her hands.

" And the prospect——" said Miss Harriet.

" Speak not of prospects, sister," said Miss Daw, severely. " I promise nothing. But if Lachlan—whose conduct has hitherto pleased us, from the period of the murder of our unfortunate rooks until our frightful drive from the Royal Oak—if he, I say, should continue to give us general satisfaction, we should not forget him—or, I mean, we should notice him, sister Ann and sister Harriet"

" Certainly we should notice him."

" I'm sure he shall have all I——" began Miss Harriet.

" Harriet!" said Miss Daw, with a majestic wave of her hand.

" Harriet!" echoed Miss Ann.

" Sisters!" said Harriet, apologetically.

Meanwhile Lachlan was thinking of the possibility of marrying Aline on a hundred a year, giving up his profession, and becoming a man of all work to his venerable aunts. He soon determined that it would not do, and politely said so.

" Roossia is so far away," said Miss Daw. " It is quite in the northern latitudes. I do not wish you to leave the country. If you object to our proposals, at least you may stay in England."

" Nearly a thousand a year, with the prospect of honour, does not often fall at one's feet, ladies," said Lachlan, "and I insure this by going to Russia."

The ladies lifted up their hands in astonishment. Just as they were beginning their comments, Captain and Mrs. Love came in.

" Aunts, here's a letter from our poor Bob," began Mrs. Love, who had evidently been weeping. The aunts put down their uplifted hands, and sat upright like three statues.

Captain Love nodded to Lachlan, in a somewhat rude manner; Mrs. Love did not speak to him.

" Our young relative here, comes to tell us that he has an appointment of a thousand a year," said Miss Daw. " You know the trite proverb, ' Perseverance generally succeeds,' and I must say he has exemplified it."

" He *has* exemplified it," said Miss Ann.

" Going as lecturer ?" growled the Captain.

" No, as engineer," said Lachlan.

" Where ?"

" To Russia."

The Captain's face brightened. "Severe climate," he said. "You'll find the winter pretty sharp. All your money will go in furs. I knew a man who had his nose so frostbitten, that he was obliged to hold it up with his handkerchief. It was as big as a plum pudding."

"I am not ambitious of that," said Lachlan. "Can I do anything for you in the North, Captain Love?"

"If you would only see after our poor Robert, Mr. Lachlan," said Mrs. Love, whose ideas of geography were not very clear. "I should be for ever obliged to you. He's sailed away from England, all for that proud, conceited, upstart young woman, Kern Lyons, who was so deceitful that she made all the young men run after her, and then jilted them for an old one, because he is a lord. I'm sure I couldn't tell what they saw in her, could you, aunts?"

"She was certainly very handsome, and quite a lady in manner and appearance," said Miss Daw.

"Certainly a lady," echoed Miss Ann.

"If you will allow me to go now, ladies, I will call again to-morrow," said Lachlan, rising.

"And give us your final decision about Roossia," said Miss Daw.

"Yes," said Lachlan, and left the room, followed by Miss Harriet.

"Don't go so far away," she said when they reached the hall. "Sisters are old, and changeable. The Manor Farm is ours to leave. It belonged to your ancestors, and so did this house, and more that we possess. I must not be more explicit; but you are the only relation I have that I love very much, and sisters begin to care for you as well."

Lachlan said he would think the matter over; and so he did: but he could not come to any decision as to whether he ought to remain in England or not.

Aline decided for him.

The following day he again went to the farm. Aline was on the watch for him, as he descended the Downs, and managed to be in the garden when he entered it. They went into the arbour and sat down there.

Aline had lost the spirits of the previous day, and looked almost sad. She told Lachlan that her mother had given her free permission to see him—as she had informed her that he was in their secret—and to give him such messages as she wished conveyed to her father. But she had not made much further way in her mother's confidence. Madam Rambully had been composed and thoughtful, and had listened to all that Aline had to say of her father. She had shown some emotion when she delivered his message, and had declared that she freely forgave him, but that she could not bring herself to meet him again, as she feared that it would be her death. She had especially begged that, as long as they were at the Downs, no disclosures should be made to any of her husband's family, concerning her and Aline. Whatever she might allow elsewhere, she could not avow herself the wife of William Eagles in the house of the parents of her who had been his first love.

Aline had fancied that some great inward change had been produced in her mamma, and that she was relenting towards her father: but she had not said so in words. Of one thing however, Aline was certain, and that was, that if they were to be eventually reconciled, they must leave the Downs Farm as soon as possible.

When Aline told Lachlan this, she began to

cry. Lachlan felt inclined to cry with her. Aline was as much a part of the Downs Farm as were daddy and granny Bull.

"I do not think I should mind leaving so much," she said, striving to recover herself, "if you were not going so far away;—if you were in London, and if we were to go there, I should feel that I had some one to advise me— some one to help me in the difficult task that must devolve upon me—but——"

"Why, dear Aline, will you not give me the right to share your troubles?" said Lachlan.

"Do not put that temptation in my way again," said Aline. "Neither my father nor mother would, I am sure, bear any one with them but me, or be dependent on any one else. My duty is wholly with them, at present. I must not rest until I bring them together, and then I must labour to keep them together, which will be a less easy task than the re-union. But oh! if you were not going so far! Yesterday I thought I could bear it, but to leave the Downs, and lose you, would be very hard indeed."

Aline looked up at Lachlan through her tears, and he made the decision I have mentioned before.

" Aline, I cannot leave you. I will not go to Russia."

A cry of joy burst from Aline. In a minute, however, she said—

" But you must not give up your prospect of advancement for me."

" Partly for you, and partly for myself. At all risks I will not go."

" Now, Lachlan, I am quite happy," said Aline, one of her sweet smiles making sunshine in her eyes and mouth. " I shall not even object to go to London, if you are there."

" At any rate I shall be there from time to time, and watch over you, my Aline. But I must now tell you a secret, which as yet I have kept to myself, as I did not quite know what to do. I have had the offer of Lord Yeominster's new bridge over the Yeo, and all the drainage and levelling connected with it, and the road over the downs. He chose mine out of the hundred plans sent in. I have been debating between this offer and Mr. Markman's, not liking to refuse anything he wished me to do: but now I am decided."

Aline clapped her hands.

"They will think you a much greater man here, if you do this work, than if you made all the railways in Russia."

"I believe I am doing right, Aline, not only as regards you, but my aunts. Although they have never done me much service, I cannot help having a liking for them, particularly Miss Harriet, who was always very kind to me. By making this bridge, I shall be able to look after their property a little. I have also another reason: so, you see, I am pulling down your vanity. My uncle is in very bad health, and I find that he has been sadly neglecting his farming. If some one does not help him he will be ruined. Kezia is the only stay they have. All the boys have the unhappy family ambition, and will not stick to farming: not, at least, in this country. John is determined to go out to Matthew, who has written to invite him, and who is doing very well in Australia. Uncle had a letter the other day, full of flourishes. He has got over Mrs. Bat's cruelty, and found another dark-eyed lady, whose name is also Ellen, to console him. I wonder whether I could ever be so consoled if you were to be cruel to me, Aline?"

"Ellen never loved Matthew," said Aline, simply.

"If John goes away, there will be only Jacob and Esau," continued Lachlan, "and I have always looked upon them as my property, ever since they were so fond of me when they were babies. Only fancy their being twelve years old, now! Mr. Eagles has grounded them well, and if I get on, I shall be able to give them a lift together. They are so fond of one another, that I think they would be wretched far apart. I remember, when they took to me that first evening, I vowed to myself to befriend them and little Rhoda, always."

"I will help you, Lachlan. Whatever you do I will do. But why do you think Mr. Lyons so ill?"

"He was never strong, and my aunt, though always complaining, has really the best health of the two. But she has wearied and worried him to death. Women have much to answer for, my Aline, when they allow their tempers to get the better of them—and do not know how to manage their husbands."

"That was mamma's difficulty," said Aline.

"I am sure she did not understand my father's temper."

"You will know better, I am sure," said Lachlan.

"I like people to do just what pleases them," said Aline. "But Mr. Lyons? You do not think he will die! Oh! that is shocking."

"He seems to me to be breaking up; and Kern's marriage, or rather the manner of it, has been a great blow to him. It evidently preys on his mind. She was his favourite daughter, and she left the country without returning home at all. He went to Brooklands to see her, and they nearly quarrelled. My uncle is as proud a man as ever lived, and does not like to be ignored as the father of his child."

"I do not think any one need be ashamed of owning Mr. Lyons for a father," said Aline.

"Nor do I. But Kern is not like you."

A shade came over Lachlan's face. He suddenly remembered, that perhaps he had had something to do with her hasty departure. He changed the subject.

"Then, Aline, there will be only Kezia and Rhoda; and if my uncle should be obliged to give up the farm, or if——Under any circumstances, they and my aunt would be provided for. It is such a relief to me to talk to you on this subject. I have not ventured to name it to any one else."

At this point of the conversation, Fluke's voice was heard, calling loudly for Aline. She rose instantly, and went to her—begging Lachlan to remain a few minutes.

"It is lucky you are near," said Fluke; "for my lady wants you imperative. How *can* you, Miss Aline?"

Aline understood the tone of reproof and disgust in which the last words were uttered.

"I *can* do what I like, Fluke, and what mamma allows."

Madam Rambully wanted Aline to give a particular message to Lachlan.

Her state of mind was as unaccountable to herself as to those about her. She had been suddenly seized by a great desire to see her husband again, and to hear, from his own lips, the truth of the statement made by Aline. But she did not wish either him, Lachlan, or Aline, to suppose that she had such a desire. Hence the seeming inconsistency of her conduct. At one moment she would say that she consented to forgive him, and perhaps to see him ; at another that she would never see him again. Her present message to Lachlan was, apparently, decisive.

" Aline," she said, " I have had a horrible dream. I thought he was dying, and that I was trying to reach him, and could not. I was tied by this stupid leg. I must end this wretched farce. Tell them to settle it as they will. I will see him again, but not here. No one in this house or neighbourhood must know of the connection between us. I can be taken from this place to some spot or other where a meeting may be managed, and then go away for ever. To London, or abroad, or anywhere out of the scenes haunted by Mary Bull. I have seen her, too; and feel as if I had murdered her. Remember, if I consent to see him once more, I can never live with him again."

Aline kissed her mother, went to Lachlan, delivered the message, and returned instantly.

Madam Rambully was greatly excited, and very ill. Fluke and Aline had as much as they could do to calm her. As the day wore on she became almost delirious, and they were obliged to give her a strong opiate to induce sleep; which came at last, to their great relief. They did not know that she had not slept at all, before, since the day on which Aline had made her disclosure concerning her father.

While she was sleeping, Fluke got Aline down into the parlour to have some tea, and in an aggrieved voice, and with a much injured manner, held forth to her, as follows:

"I suppose, Miss Aline, although you are trying all you can to shut up my 'art, you don't imagine you can shut my eyes and ears. As I have been in all my lady's secrets till now, it seems unnatural to be shut out of this one; though I may as well tell you 'tis no secret at all, for I have known it long before you did. 'Owever, *you* have *your* friends, and you don't want me. ' New brooms sweep clean.' I 'ope your Lacklands will sweep better than I have, that's all I can say."

"Now, Fluke, you are very unjust," said Aline, with a little twinge of conscience.

"No, I am not, Miss Aline—at least I expect more than I get, or perhaps than I have any right to get. I, a poor foundling with nobody but you and your mamma in the world.”

A tear crept into Fluke’s eye.

Simultaneously, a dozen tears burst into Aline’s. She had her arms round Fluke’s neck in a moment.

“My dear old Fluke! my darling old Fluke! You know I love you dearly; next to mamma; only there are some things so sacred that one cannot talk of them.”

“I know—I know,” said Fluke, now fairly breaking down, and sobbing, “I expect too much. But you might have told me about Mr. Eagles, and asked my advice. I shouldn’t have let your mamma come to this pass. I know she has been dying for him ever since she broke her leg, and ’eard he was so ill; only her pride held her back. Women are so foolish! You are all alike! And now your turn is come,—and such a come-down, too!”

“Do you mean, Fluke, that mamma has really been anxious to see my father?” said Aline.

“Father, indeed! I beg your pardon, miss; but it *do* seem so odd. Yes. She always worshipped the ground he trod on; it was only pride and jealousy that got the better of love at last. Pity they 'adn't continued to do so. I never see any one suffer as she did after he left her, or she left him, whichever it was. It was crying after they parted, that made her blind — not crying before they parted."

" Then my task is easy," said Aline.

" I could have told you so from the first, if you had consulted me. It will be easy enough to bring 'em together, but not so easy to keep 'em together. Like a pair of scissors— when the rivet has once come out, 'tis always coming out, put it in again as often as you will. You're making a pretty bed for yourself and every bodyelse."

" I can lie on it, Fluke."

CHAPTER IX.

WE LEAVE THE DOWNS FARM.

As Aline was declaring her intention of lying on the bed she had made, Mrs. Bat entered the parlour, unannounced. Fluke made a hasty exit. She never liked any of the Eagles family, and never meant to like them.

"At last!" exclaimed Ellen, throwing her arms round Aline, and hugging her. "Don't be frightened—I know everything! I am your aunt, and you are my dear, dear niece— my only brother's only child. I always knew we were related, or I could never have loved you so well!"

Aline hugged Mrs. Bat until you would have thought they were bears; and then began to cry and laugh together, and then hugged her again.

"Is it not delightful? How did you know it? Who could have told you? Not Lachlan?"

When Aline's excitement was a little subdued, Ellen told her how she had heard the wonderful news.

We must remember that William Eagles paid his first visit to his sister the previous day. She and her husband prevailed on him to sleep at the Lodge, and sent for their father to complete the family party. Nothing that his friends could do or say, could arouse William Eagles from his abstraction and melancholy, except any chance allusion to the Downs Farm or its inmates; and Ellen began to fear that her brother had really fallen in love with Aline.

When Lachlan left Aline that morning, he went in search of William Eagles, and found him at the Lodge. He and Ellen were together. Lachlan begged for a few minutes' private conversation, and Ellen said she hoped they were not going to fight a duel for Aline.

When Lachlan had delivered the message with which he was charged, William had at once said, " I must tell my sister—come with me to her."

They went to Ellen, accordingly.

" Tell her all—I cannot," said William ; and Lachlan told the story of his Aline and her father, as shortly and clearly as he could. William Eagles left the room as soon as he began, and was nowhere to be found when he ended.

Ellen's astonishment may be imagined. For a time she could not believe the tale ; but when she was convinced of its truth, like a loyal wife, and with her natural impetuosity, she ran away from Lachlan in search of her husband, to communicate to him the wondrous history.

" I will never tell a married woman anything again," thought Lachlan ; who waited for her return until he was tired, and then went his way.

" And now, Aline," said Ellen, " I am come to see your mother, and to tell her that she must come at once to the Lodge. Oliver and I settled it all in half an hour. There is no other place in or out of the parish where they can meet ; and there they can do so in strict privacy. Even my father and brothers-in-law need know nothing of the secret. Go and tell her at once, and say that I hope for an interview."

Aline went.

"Mamma, Mrs. Bat is here," she said to her mother, trembling for the result of the intelligence.

"Mrs. Bat! What can she want? I never wish to see her again, or any of the family, except your father."

"She is so anxious to see you, dear mother. She knows all, and she comes as a sister."

"Nonsense. She never liked me. How could he have told her? Now every one will hear the story, and I shall be the butt of all the gossips."

"No one will hear it, mamma, unless you wish. She will do everything you like. She only asks to see you. She came the very moment she had heard who you really were, and is so glad that we are here."

"That is the very worst part of the whole affair, Aline. I do not want any new relations."

"But see her, dear mother. She came so

soon. In all the joy and kindness of her heart: and I love her so very dearly. For my sake, at least."

"I am so unprepared. What can she want?"

"She will tell you herself. May I bring her up?"

"Very well, but you must take all the consequences of the excitement."

Ellen soon made her appearance. She was really the most excited of the two. She hurried to the sofa on which was her new sister, and instead of taking the cold, thin hand, languidly put out, threw her arms round her, and gave her an affectionate kiss, the first she had ever given her. Then she knelt down, and taking her hand, began to talk rapidly. Although Madam Rambully could not see the tears in her black eyes, she could hear that her voice was broken by emotion.

"I am so glad, so very glad. I have such a great esteem for you, and such a love for Aline, that nothing on earth could have given me greater joy. Will you let me love you, and will you try to love me as a sister? Pride kept me from seeking your love when I was

Aline's governess, because I thought you would not give it to me, but now I may claim it almost as my due. And he—my poor brother—he, too, has a claim to advance. Do not resist it. He is dying, more from anxiety and uncertainty than from disease. He asks for a reunion with you, and a share in Aline. He knows that he has grievously sinned, but he hopes not past forgiveness by his heavenly Judge, and therefore not quite unpardonably by you, his earthly one."

"I forgive him," murmured the trembling wife, striving for mastery over her feelings, " but——"

"Do not qualify your forgiveness, but see him first. If you will only fall into my plans you will make us all so happy. You must come at once to us. My husband will be very glad to see you, and to become known to the mother of his dear Aline: and my brothers, too, will welcome you for her sake. They shall not know the secret. You must come as a visitor—nay, do not refuse. I will send the carriage for you. Mrs. Fluke can come with you. You can even keep to your own room if you like. William shall not know anything

about it until you wish.   Dear, dear sister, for
all our sakes, consent."

Ellen kissed the hand she held, and Aline
fell on her knees at the other side of the sofa,
and throwing her arm over her mother, said—

"Darling mother, make us all happy.   Be
happy once more yourself.   After so many
years of secrecy and misery be your own self
again."

The agitated mother lost all power of restraint, and burst into tears and sobs.

"Thank you—a thousand times thank you,"
she said, in a broken voice.   "But he does not
love me.   He never, never loved me."

"See him!   Let him speak for himself,"
cried Ellen.   "Say you will come to us, and
all will be well.   To-morrow, at two o'clock, I
will send the carriage for you.   I will positively
take no refusal, and Aline and Mrs. Fluke will
manage everything for you.   The change will
do your health good, and you shall not see my
brother until you wish.   I will not excite you
any longer, for I am sure you cannot bear it."

Ellen rose, and bent over Mrs. Eagles (as
we must at last call her), and kissed her flushed,
damp cheek.   Mrs. Eagles rose with an effort,

and putting her arms round her, returned the sisterly embrace with fervour.

"I thank you, I thank you," she said, trying to repress her sobs. "Whatever may be the end of all this, I shall never forget your kindness. I cannot promise for to-morrow, but Aline shall let you know. Although my heart has been crushed by many years of sorrow, it may regain some feeling, and learn to love you as—as—a sister."

"Dear, darling mother!" said Aline, kissing her hand, and letting her tears fall upon it.

Ellen, who was not given to weeping, hastened out of the room, and thence out of the house, to let the fresh air of the Downs dry hers, which would fall in spite of herself. Mother and daughter forgot the danger of those tears to the precious sight of the former, but let them flow a while, unrepressed.

"Aline, I will go," said Mrs. Eagles, after a long silence. "It is the best plan of all. Send Fluke to me, and prepare Mr. and Mrs. Bull for this extraordinary move. I do not think I shall ever come back to this place again."

This sudden resolution startled Aline. She did not know that her mother was longing for any feasible plan of seeing her husband, and already panted for the morrow.

Fluke had no easy service the rest of that day. Mrs. Eagles had the whole of her wardrobe brought forth, and examined it minutely. She appeared to be satisfied with nothing. One dress was old-fashioned, another vulgar, a third unbecoming, a fourth shabby, and so on. Mantles, bonnets, gloves even shared the same fate. In vain Fluke pleaded for one article of dress, or Aline for another—none was satisfactory. The jewelry was more fortunate, inasmuch as it was all real and good. Aline, who scarcely ever remembered to have seen her mother wear an ornament, was astonished to find that dressing-cases and jewel-boxes were turned inside out for diamonds and turquoises— her mother's favourite stones.

"If I could but see!" was her incessant cry, as Fluke fidgeted over one thing and another, and utterly failed to please her mistress: and Aline was not more successful.

There was no time for any new purchases, so they were obliged to make the best of the materials they possessed. Aline tried to be useful, but was at last told, both by mistress and maid, that she was in the way. Her evident surprise and amusement at the sudden change in her mother rather annoyed that lady. She was conscious that for the last fifteen years she had been quite careless about her dress, putting on whatever Fluke chose, provided the prevailing colour were blue, and the whole ladylike and good; but now she was equally conscious of a sudden return to the fastidiousness of her girlhood, and felt half ashamed that Aline should witness the change.

Fluke, originally a first-rate dressmaker, had with difficulty kept pace with the times; still she was not far behind them. As she said, she did not go to church, and once a month to Yeominster for nothing. She never returned without a new pattern vividly painted on her eye, and transferable, at pleasure, to whatever she was manufacturing in the way of dress. In this way she kept "her ladies up to the mark," as she expressed it; and intractable as Aline was on week days—persisting in wearing sun-bonnets and pinafores till Fluke was ashamed of her—she made, what that excellent Abigail called, a decently fashionable appearance on Sundays.

"Now Miss Aline," she said, as Aline was enjoying a hearty laugh at her and her mother's expense, "if instead of irritating your mamma and provoking me, you would just run across to Yeo, and ask Miss Leech to lend me her last book of fashions, you would be of some use. I know she had one two or three months back, and she would do anything on earth for you. If you had no objections, my lady, she might come herself, and 'elp to run up an evening dress for Miss Aline."

"I don't want an evening dress, Fluke. I should feel ashamed of myself in a low body."

"Do go, Aline," said Mrs. Eagles; "you must not shame your new relations. You needn't wear a low body if you dislike it; but you might get that dress you had for Mrs. Bat's wedding made wearable."

"It is quite wearable now, mamma, but I will go if you wish it."

"Do ask Miss Leech to bring over anything she can find in Roe's shop worth looking at. Ribbons particular. You're not going out for the first time, Miss Aline, such a show as you make of yourself here."

Off went Aline, her eyes dancing with merriment, and certainly her mother and Fluke did much better without her.

Miss Leech lived on the outskirts of the village, and Aline had won her heart by kindness to her sick mother; so no sooner was her errand made known, than Miss Leech left a dress that she was making, and started for Roe's shop.

When Aline returned to the farm, she found that Fluke had enlisted Kezia Lyons in the service, who had come over to see her grandmother, and even that excellent old woman had some sort of employment thrust upon her before nightfall. Aline, also, was compelled to assist, so the work went bravely on, and by twelve o'clock the following day, Fluke had achieved a very presentable wardrobe for her "ladies."

Mr. and Mrs. Bull were so surprised at this unexpected visit, that they could scarcely believe in it at all. Aline told them that they were going to spend a few days at the Lodge, and Mrs. Bull's uplifted hands, and her exclamation of "Well, to be sure, wonders *will* never cease," were received by her with such glee, that the old couple could only rejoice in the happiness of their darling.

"Dear heart!" said Mrs. Bull, "it does one good to see her. She hasn't been so gleesome for many a day. She is dancing and singing about just as she used to be ; and the house is as cheerful like, as if the sun was beginning to shine after a long rain."

"God bless her !" echoed the farmer.

"She was never one to be long cast down. She was born one of God's blessings ; bright herself, and to make other folk bright. But what has stirred up madam I can't think. And Mrs. Fluke, too, as busy as a hen in the dawning, and Mrs. Bat coming here in that sudden sort of way, there's more in the wind than we can see, grammer, be you sure."

"The Lord grant it's for missey's good, granfer. Madam has been walking about her room half the day. There was no moving her before. The doctors said she wanted some strong stimulant——"

"Stimulus, you mean, granny. I never knew you so scandalous before as to say madam had taken to drinking."

"Well, 'tis a comfort that you can always

have your joke. They said her nerves were just as much broken as her leg, and that she could walk well enough if she'd a mind. The will was wanting. And now, I suppose, she has found the stimulant, but what the Mr. Bats will do with her, I can't conceive."

"Why the old gen'leman 'll show her his crops, and Nick 'll run away, and Oliver 'll wish her farther, and the gossips 'll have another nine days' wonder, besides Kern's marriage."

"Don't talk o' that, granfer, it makes me poorly like."

"Humph! My grandson, the earl! It sounds well for Farmer and Mrs. Bull. Rhoda clucks about like a bantam that has hatched a young turkey. The slut! she was always above her station."

"But you know, the Lyonses are——"

"My dear, I've known ever since I was in swaddling clothes. Lachlan's the best I've seen of 'em. I wish she'd married Lachlan. But then missey couldn't have had 'un ; so all's best as it is."

Even Aline was obliged to confess that the

"stimulus" had done wonders for her mother. She was able to walk with her or Fluke's assistance, and even her sight seemed improved. Fluke insinuated to Aline what the doctors had previously said, that if her mamma had really wished to recover, she might have done so, and that although she professed to desire to leave the farm, some stronger inclination kept her there.

"'Tis to be hoped that something will keep her going, now she is set off," said Fluke. "She has been down long enough, thanks to entertaining that depressing, nonsensical passion they call love. Why I believe she was most in love when she said that she 'ated him most! Thank 'eaven! I was never overcome by such trash."

"I hope they will be happy at last," said Aline, feeling how uncertain the future still was.

At the appointed hour the carriage arrived from the Lodge, and all the farm servants were astir to look at it. Madam Rambully going out at last, and to pay a visit to the Bats! This was an event! There were eyes peeping through the kitchen window, staring out of the barns and cow-sheds, blinking at every gate that was to be kept open, and gazing from the front door.

Here stood Mr. and Mrs. Bull, Kezia, and Miss Leech, all expectant, together with the servants from the Downs Lodge, also expectant.

When the party appeared, the surprise was great.   Madam Rambully was quite changed. She had suddenly turned into a young and fashionable woman, and blindness and lameness were apparently thrown aside.   True, she leaned on Aline's arm for support and guidance, but a stranger would not have known why. The large blue shade was gone from the eyes, and in its place was a profusion of curls, and a face flushed like the morning.   She was still dressed in blue, but no longer to conceal the elegance of her figure and the pale beauty of her face, but to heighten their attractions. Even Aline gazed on her mother with astonishment.   Not so Fluke.   She carried her shawls and dressing-case with the proud consciousness of being once more in her right place, and nodded to her friends with the air of a proper waiting-woman, attending on a proper mistress.

Mrs. Eagles pressed the hands of Mr. and Mrs. Bull, as she hurried past them, but did not speak.

"Mamma cannot say good-bye," said Aline, returning hastily, after she had helped her mother into the carriage; "I will come back again to-morrow if I can."

Tears came into her eyes. She kissed her daddy and granny hastily, and shook hands with the rest, to the no small surprise of the servants of the Downs Lodge.

"Dear heart, God bless her!" said Mrs. Bull, her ready tears flowing for company.

"There's more in the wind than we know of," said farmer Bull, as they stood watching the carriage as it rolled over the grass. "Madam is covering her eyes, and missey waving her pretty hand, just as if they were going away for good."

"That would break the darling's heart," said Mrs. Bull, turning to go into the house, as the carriage disappeared in the trees beyond the chapel.

"God bless her! God for ever bless her,

wherever she goes!" said the good farmer, extending his hands towards the spot where he had last seen the carriage. " Don't cry, Kezia lass ; one 'ud think they were going away for ever."

CHAPTER X.

THE INTERVIEW.

When the carriage reached the door of the Downs Lodge, Ellen, alone, was there to receive her guests. She embraced them in silence, and hurried them at once to their room.

"A thousand welcomes," she said, as she again kissed them both, and tried to gain some degree of composure.

"Let it be over as soon as you can," said Mrs. Eagles. "If he is in the house let me see him at once."

She began, nervously, to try and unfasten the strings of her bonnet. Aline did it for her.

"If I might be left with Fluke for five minutes," she said.

Mrs. Bat and Aline quitted the room.

Fluke took off her mistress's shawl, arranged her hair, assured her that she looked as beautiful and almost as young as she did more than twenty years ago, and finally recalled Mrs. Bat and Aline.

The former took her guests to her morning-room, which was nearly close to their rooms, and insisted on her sister-in-law's taking a glass of wine. Mrs. Eagles trembled so much that she could scarcely hold the glass.

"Is he here?" she asked. "If I do not get it over now, I shall never be able to see him."

"Dear mamma—not so soon," said the agitated Aline.

"Now or never," was the reply.

"May I stay, dear mother?" asked Aline.

"I must be alone," was the decided answer.

Ellen, almost as much agitated as her newly-found relatives, gently placed her sister in an easy chair, near a comfortable fire. Then she kissed her forehead, and taking Aline's hand, drew her from the room.

"It will kill her," said Aline.

"No, it will not. Your father is in the library; we will fetch him."

They found William Eagles pacing up and down the library, in so excited a state, that had they not entered just then, he would have gone in search of them.

Aline threw her arms round him, and said—

"Be gentle with her. If she is proud—or harsh—or unforgiving—bear with her. Father, dear father, bear with her, or she will die."

"I will—I will. Only let me see her, and be forgiven, and I will go away for ever."

This was always the burden of his tale.

Aline led her father up-stairs. Such care had been taken by Mr. and Mrs. Bat to get the household out of the way that they did not meet any one.

Aline pointed to the door.

"Open it—I cannot," said her father.

She did so, and closed it after him. Ellen met her on the landing, and taking her into her own bedroom, which was next to the room in which she had left her parents, comforted and sustained her as best she could.

William Eagles stood, motionless, by the door which Aline had shut behind him; his wife sat opposite him, shading her eyes from the light. She heard the door open, but it was too far from her to allow her imperfect sight to realize the in-comer. Something dark was all that she perceived, and so she thought that no one had entered.

"He will not come," she murmured.

"He will—he will," said her husband, still standing by the door, unable to move towards her.

She did not recognize the hoarse voice.

"Then why not at once—at once?" she said.

He made a great effort, and staggered towards her.

She gave a little cry when she knew that it was really he; her hands fell into her lap, and she nearly fainted. His failing health and excited mind made him almost as weak as she was; but seeing her momentary prostration when he expected the severe strength of the never-forgotten interview at Venice, he roused himself. He forgot the humble speech that he had been so long rehearsing to himself, the humble position he had meant to take, on his knees—at her feet; he saw her head droop, as she, too, forgot, in the weakness of the moment, the calm dignity with which she had intended to receive him, and with a loud cry of " Aline ! Aline ! I have killed her !" he put his arms round her to support the sinking head, pressed his lips on the closing eyes, and felt an agony of love and remorse, great as even that deserted wife could have desired.

But the eyes opened, and before he could think or speak, her arms were round his neck, and her lips returning the kisses he was giving.

Aline, who had heard the wild cry, entered at this moment, as it was right she should. She, who had effected this meeting, thus witnessed its blessed consummation. She ran towards them, saw that all was as she had prayed it should be, and, falling on her knees at her mother's feet, she hid her face in her lap, and let her tears have way.

"Forgive me, forgive me, my love! my wife!" at last said William Eagles.

"I do! I do!" said his wife. "Only tell me you really love me."

"God knows I love you! I only meant to

—ask forgiveness—and to leave you for ever; but now——"

"Leave me? What, again?"

"Never—never!" said Aline, rising. "You will never part again as long as you live. Bless me, kiss me, now that you are together, mother, father!"

Part again! No; they could never part again with that sweet Aline as a bond of union. They kissed her; they blessed her; and again and again embraced one another. Pure, natural love sprang up from the long-closed founts; and the husband and wife who parted in scorn, hate, and misery, met with an affection unknown before, nurtured by that filial love so strong in Aline. All the abject self-abasement, unnaturally intended by him whom God made to command, and all the proud self-respect intended by her whom God created to obey, melted away in the presence of the child whom that same great Being had created pure, simple, and steadfast in well-doing. Nature resumed her rights, and husband and wife, parent and child, inwardly vowed to do their best towards the fulfilment of Aline's prophetic words.

Again Aline fell upon her knees at her mother's side. In the simple earnestness of her young heart, she felt that one thing was yet wanting to make that union perfect.

"Let us ask God to bless us," she said; "and then He will not let us part again."

"May He indeed have mercy upon us, and forgive us our sins, and help us to do our duty," said William, solemnly, laying his hand on his wife's head, as she bent over Aline.

"And put into our hearts His new commandment, that 'we love one another,'" concluded Aline, raising her tearful eyes to heaven, and then letting them rest on her parents.

There was a moment of prayerful silence, during which a Divine ray entered the hearts of William Eagles and his wife, which had never pierced so far before. It showed them their sin, and how alone it was to be forgiven.

Then Aline rose from her knees, and quietly left the room. She knew that others were anxiously awaiting the result of those first words, and she must make them as happy as herself. Ellen and Fluke were together, eagerly listening for any sound. Fluke was just comforting Mrs. Bat by assuring her that "an angel from 'eaven would never keep them from quarrelling" when Aline appeared.

"All is right—they are never going to part again," she said, giving way to her emotion.

"I dare say not," muttered the unmanageable Fluke, catching Aline in her arms, as if she were, as she believed her to be, a great deal more her property than Mrs. Bat's. "And now, do stop crying, Miss Aline,"—Fluke had great difficulty to keep from it herself,—"and don't spoil your eyes; you know they're the only good feature in your face, and they're looking a sight."

"Aline, dear child, I must go and tell Oliver," said the loyal wife; "I shall be back directly."

Fluke was delighted, and abandoned herself to scolding Aline into repose as soon as Ellen was gone.

"You cross, cruel, unkind, dear old Fluke!" said Aline, wiping away her tears. "If you only knew what it is to feel that one has two parents, and that they will never part again."

"Thank 'eaven that I don't," said Fluke.

"As I never 'ad any parents I don't know the loss of 'em; and I don't see what good they are, for my part. I dare say I shouldn't be 'alf so respectable, or 'appy either, if I 'ad any. I've nobody to bother me but you now; and you're enough, goodness knows."

"Oh, Fluke!" said Aline, "you are not at all glad. I am quite ashamed of you, you disagreeable old Fluke!'

"There! now you are my dear child again. It does my 'eart good to 'ear those pleasant old names. And I really am tolerably glad, because you are glad. But you'll 'ave bother enough between 'em, poor dear! However, I'll stand by and 'elp. I'm not going away for all the Eagles or Aquiles—faugh!—under 'eaven."

"I should think not, Fluke! We shall be as happy as the day. No more deceit. I feel as light as air already, and wish I were up on the Downs with Max, running a race. Where is Max?"

"He ran away after Lachlan. He's fonder of Lachlan than you."

"Indeed he is not. Hush! I hear a sound! I hope mamma is not crying."

"Fiddle-de-dee! They'll bill and coo for a day or so, and then——"

Aline put her hand over Fluke's mouth, and stood in an attitude of attention.

"Only to think of this grand room belonging to——" began Fluke, resolved to withdraw Aline's thoughts from what was passing so near her: "I beg your pardon, Miss Eagles. Law! I shall never be able to say *that*—belonging to your aunt! 'Wonders 'll never cease while miracles are in fashion,' as Mr. Bull says."

"You are quite right, Mrs. Fluke," said Mr. Oliver Bat, who entered the room with his wife while Fluke was enunciating one of farmer Bull's favourite saws. "Allow me to renew our old acquaintance as Aline's uncle. I hope I may claim a little portion of the general darling now, though you wouldn't let me years ago. May I kiss her, and shake hands with you?"

"That you may, sir," said Fluke, heartily; " for you, at least, are a true gentleman."

Mr. Oliver did both.

"And now, Aline, we will have another canter on the Downs," said Oliver. " The last time you were here, you helped me to a good wife, and now I hope I have helped you to a good father. In the old days I scarcely believed in such *rara aves*, but I am getting old, and age makes one silly. Aline, unless the servants are all to be in the secret, you must break up the *tête-à-tête* in the next room. We caught the housemaid on the stairs. Ask them if I may come in?"

"Not yet," said Ellen.

"It will be better to get it all over at once, —don't you think so, Mrs. Fluke? I take it that you and I are the only pair blessed with common sense of the party."

"Certainly, sir. My lady will cry her eyes out, if they are left much longer. And you would cheer her up a little."

Aline went to her parents. She found them seated close together, apparently in loving but painful conversation, for her mother had her handkerchief to her eyes, and her father seemed still to be confessing his sins."

"Do not interrupt us, Aline," said her mother.

"Dear mamma, Mr. Oliver Bat asks if he may be introduced to you, and says that unless you wish everything made known at once, you had better not remain here longer alone together."

"Let him come in, *anima mia*. Anything but to separate us, even for an hour. He will not annoy you," said William Eagles.

"It is ungentlemanlike—it is too soon," said his wife.

"Perhaps he thinks as the servants have found out that you have seen papa, you had better see him also."

"He is right, *carina*," said William.

"Then let them all come and look at me, and go away again."

Aline soon returned with Mr. and Mrs. Oliver Bat. As the former had occasionally seen Mrs. Eagles before, and spoken to her, the introduction was merely nominal. "I am very glad to welcome you to the Lodge," he said, purposely avoiding giving her any name. "Aline has so long had a warm corner in all our hearts, that my brothers will be equally glad to see you. And now we shall have a chance of chaining *this* brother to the eyrie, since he has found so lovely a mate in it."

Mr. Oliver put his hand kindly on William's shoulder.

"Thank you, *mon ami*," said William, who, when quite himself, always used foreign terms of endearment.

"Ellen and I think—or more properly that inimitable Mrs. Fluke and I think"—continued Oliver, "that you will need rest after your drive, and I propose running away with William until dinner time."

"I cannot appear—you will excuse me," said Mrs. Eagles.

"Certainly. You must make yourself quite at home. Perhaps you will be able to join us after dinner in the drawing-room. My brothers will be most anxious to see you, particularly Nicholas."

Mr. Oliver could not help casting a sly glance at Ellen, for he had been working hard half the morning, to persuade that shy brother into appearing at all.

Even Mrs. Eagles smiled, for she had heard of "Nervous Nick" from Kern.

"I am afraid I am intruding," she said. "I would not for the world—I—we—shall leave immediately for London, I hope."

The effort at speech being made, Mr. Oliver found his work easier.

"Ellen will not hear of your leaving us yet. We mean to keep you for a long time."

"As long as you like," said Ellen. "Only think yourself at home, and with friends who love you."

"That abominable novel-writing made Ellen so sentimental," said Mr. Oliver; "she must say 'with friends who love you,' when all that is taken for granted by matter-of-fact people. Come along, William. Don't you see we are intruding?"

William bent over his wife and whispered that he would return soon, called Oliver a tyrant, and left the room with him and Ellen.

"Aline, where are you?" said Mrs. Eagles.

"Here, mamma."

"Who is in the room?"

"Only I, mamma."

"Do you think he really means to come again, or will he go away, as he said at first? I have been so often deceived that I scarcely dare to believe."

"I am sure that he will do what you wish,

dear mother, and that you will never part again."

"My darling; what should I do without you? My heart would have broken long ago; and now it seems breaking from this sudden happiness."

"You really love him, dearest mother?"

"Ah yes! I love him. If I only could believe that he loved me as I do him, there would be no no more doubt or fear. I have never ceased to love him. When I tried to hate, it was only another phase of love. He has been between me and God, I loved him so passionately. And now it is all come back, and he may deceive me again. He is not changed. Aline. His voice and manner are what they were when I first met him; and his hand is as soft and tender as then. I could not see his face, but am sure it, too, is the same. Could it be possible that we could also love again, as we did so long ago? I could forget and forgive all the past, if I were only sure of this. Do you think he could love me now as then?"

"Perhaps better, dear mamma; for you have both seen trouble."

"And—and—that other—the unfortunate Mary—she cannot come between us now. But, Aline, we must go away from this place. I told him so, and he agreed with me. And we must leave immediately, before anyone knows who and what we are. I could not endure a general *dénouement* while we are in the country."

"Oh, mamma! How can we exist else-where?"

"Perfectly well, Aline. In London we can live as we like—at all events we will go first to London. ·I have resolved upon that."

"Lachlan is going to London,—that would make it pleasanter; Kern will be in London, Dr. and Mrs. Dove, and Mark and Luke. I should not dislike London for a little time, and then, when the gossip is over, we can return to Yeo."

"That may or may not be, Aline, but a change will be good for you."

"I shall never be so happy anywhere, dear mother, as here. I should wish to live and die among the Downs."

"Nonsense. But you must dress for dinner: There is the bell. It seems like new life to hear a dinner-bell again. Go to Fluke, dear; I wish to be alone for a few minutes to try to realize this strange dream."

Aline did as she was bid, and while Fluke was putting on that same white dress that she had worn at her aunt's marriage, she thought and spoke with infinite pain of the prospect of quitting the Downs.

When she and Ellen left the dining-room, after dinner, they went to fetch Mrs. Eagles into the drawing-room. They found her looking so youthful and elegant, that Aline scarcely knew her own mother. A rich light-blue silk dress, a black lace shawl of Brussels manufacture, and a head-dress of black lace and pearls, set off the pale fair face, and complexion wonderfully. Fluke had attired her to her own perfect satisfaction, and when Aline threw her arms round her and exclaimed, "Darling mother! you look lovely! No wonder papa fell in love with you," that worthy woman was much gratified.

" Do you think he will find me very much aged, Aline? He saw me first in blue—it was his favourite colour—that is why I have always worn it."

Ellen looked at Mrs. Eagles with wonder. Could she be the same woman whom she had seen but yesterday lying hopeless and helpless on the sofa at the farm?

They placed her by the fire in the drawing-room, in the easiest of chairs, by the most delicious of nosegays, amidst books, pictures, and all the luxuries from which, to a certain extent, she had been so long debarred.

She pressed her sister-in-law's hand, and said, "I do feel at home. I have not felt thus before since I married, three-and-twenty years ago. After all, there is nothing like the comforts of an English fireside."

Aline sat at her mother's feet on a low stool, and she, too, felt strangely at home in the warm, comfortable drawing-room, though she never remembered to have sat in such an one before.

There was a barking in the hall of many dogs.

"That is Max!" said Aline. "The other dogs will hurt him."

She was in the hall in a moment, calling her pet, where she encountered Lachlan. Mr. Bat senior had asked him to dinner, but he had not been able to come early enough.

"It is all right," cried Aline.

"Thank God!" said Lachlan, and followed her into the drawing-room.

The rest of the gentlemen were there before he had greeted Mrs. Eagles.

The large screen which she held between her face and the fire, did not suffice to conceal the flush that mounted to her temples as they came in.

"Allow me to introduce my brothers," said Mr. Oliver, still avoiding giving her a name.

"Very glad to welcome you to the Lodge, Madam Rambully," said Mr. Bat. "Your little girl has made us half acquainted with you long ago."

He took her hand and shook it heartily.

Nicholas, meanwhile, walked slowly round one table, then another, and finally meandered about behind her chair.

"This is Mr. Nicholas, who sent you the trout so often," said Aline, bringing the shrinking beau round.

"Very glad—great pleasure," he murmured, bowing before the blind lady, who put out her hand just where her husband was standing. . He grasped it eagerly, and whispered, "*mana mia*," as she was about to withdraw it. The flush deepened, and poor Nicholas withdrew in haste.

"Mamma, you did not speak to Mr. Nicholas."

"I beg your pardon. I did not see you clearly," she said, turning her graceful head round.

"Don't name it—don't name it," said the alarmed Nicholas.

"Well, Lachlan, what have the old ladies done?" broke in Mr. Bat, while William Eagles sat down by his wife and began to talk to her in Italian.

"Resisted to the death, sir; and at last I persuaded the directors to take the other cut, which was just as good, and they reign triumphant."

"And you reign in their hearts triumphant. You'll be the heir, after all."

"I ardently hope so," said Ellen.

"See how Nick is gazing at Madam Rambully," said Oliver, aside. "We shall have him in love with her. How very pretty she is! We must tell them the story to-morrow. This secresy is so awkward."

"Think of Lachlan, heir of all the Daw pro- perty, Madam Rambully," said Mr. Bat. "You don't know his respectable aunts. We'll have 'em here, Nelly, to meet Madam Rambully. The truth is, Nelly can't bear them, and Nick, and Nol, and I are such slaves to our ty- rannical mistress that we are obliged to give in to her. You remember what a tyrant she used to be, Aline?"

"Never, never!" cried Aline.

"Oh, to hear you play and sing once more!" said William to his wife. "Ellen, come here. Did you ever hear her play? Ask her to play?"

Ellen asked Mrs. Eagles to play, and she consented at once. William led her to the piano, and sat down beside her.

"Well," said Mr. Bat, "if he isn't the coolest fellow I ever saw. Met her to-day, and takes possession of her. Why, Aline, I was beginning to think of becoming your stepfather, and I am superseded already."

Mrs. Eagles played divinely. It was as if she was inspired. William listened, his pale thin face kindled, his breast heaved with emo- tion, and his wife completed the conquest that was uncompleted twenty years before.

CHAPTER XI.

FARMER BULL'S FORGIVENESS.

ALINE'S loving heart was not yet satisfied. She had brought about a reconciliation between her parents, she must now complete her work. The next morning she prevailed on her father to walk with her over the Downs, and gradually led him to the chapel near the farm. When there she said, abruptly—

"Now I must go to see daddy and granny, and you must wait for me here."

"Say once more, *ma bien aimée*, before we part, that you really believe that your mother loves me."

"I am sure of it."

"In spite of these hollow cheeks, and haggard eyes; this attenuated form, and hoarse voice.

I am so different from what I once was, *ma mie*, that even you would not have known me."

" Ah! but she does not see the change. She says you are just the same, only gentler and kinder, and she feels as if she could trust you better."

" She can—she can. Oh, blessed blindness !"

Aline hurried to the farm. She said that she must see Mr. and Mrs. Bull at once, and set off in search of the farmer, who came soon ; the latter was at hand.

She kissed the good old man, and holding his brown hand caressingly, said—

" Daddy and granny, I am come to ask the greatest favour that I ever asked of you."

" And what is that, honey ?" said the farmer. " It must be a wonderful thing, indeed, if I could refuse it thee."

" I want you to forgive Mr. William Eagles !"

" Forgive William Eagles ? Never ! What have you to do with William Eagles ?" said farmer Bull, his open brow contracting into a stern frown.

"He is my father, daddy, and you *must* forgive him, for my sake."

"Thy father, lass! What fool's nonsense art saying to an old man? I never heard thee tell a story before; don't begin now."

His voice became as stern as his face, and he withdrew his hand from Aline's.

"Do not be angry, daddy. I tell you the truth. William Eagles is my father. Granny, you will believe me, if he will not. You will forgive him, for my sake, if daddy won't."

"I have forgiven him long ago, child. But what do you mean?"

"He married my mother under the name of Signor d'Aquile, soon after he left Yeo, three or four and twenty years ago."

"The scoundrel!" growled farmer Bull.

"Oh, daddy! for my sake. They went abroad, and—and—separated."

"The heartless villain!" again interjected the farmer.

"Hush, granfer!" said his wife.

"Mamma took the name of Rambully, and we came to England. Her eyes were bad, and she had heard *him*—*my* father, daddy—once speak of Dr. Dove——"

" How dare he ?—the shameless vagabond !"

" And she went to him, and tried to find out if he knew Signor d'Aquile."

" Ha! ha! the deceiver was ashamed of his name, and well he might be."

" It is only the Italian for Eagles."

" Sure enough Italian Eagles might a' done it; English Eagles, never !"

" And Dr. Dove, by God's own guidance, daddy, sent us down here, where in course of time, *he* came,—also by God's guidance, dear daddy,—and where he has found us."

Aline's voice faltered. She put her hand on the farmer's arm, as he was pacing up and down the room.

" Forgive him, for my sake, dear daddy, and if not for mine, for God's sake, who has made him penitent, and sent him back to mamma."

" Child, I never can."

" Sit down, daddy, and listen to me. You must. There, in the old arm-chair by the fire, just as you used to do, and let me sit once more upon your knee, like a little child."

The farmer obeyed, mechanically, and Aline placed herself as she said. Mrs. Bull stood

near, looking at the window, with her handkerchief to her eyes.

"Daddy," began Aline, fixing her sweet,
tearful eyes on the farmer, and putting her
arm round his neck, "do you remember that
for many years, evening after evening, you
nursed me so, and taught me all the good
things contained in God's holy Word?   I owe
to you and granny all my love for that best
book, and such religion as I have.   When I
came here, the only right thing I knew was an
instinctive love for mamma.   From you I learnt
my duty to her.   You taught me *why* I should
be truthful and honest, why I should keep the
Sabbath, why I should speak ill of no man,
why I should be contented in my present lot,
and why I should love my neighbour as
myself.   Lachlan, and Kezia, and I, all say
that we learnt what is best from you and
granny."

"Thank God for that!" murmured Mrs.
Bull, while her husband remained silent.

" And, above all, you taught me what you
said was the most difficult lesson of all, to forgive and love my enemies.   I remember the very
evening, dear daddy.   Kern had done some-

thing to trouble me—I forget what it was—but I know it had made mamma cross with me, and you found out that I was angry. I said that I did not know why Kern was my enemy, and I would not love her any more. You asked me to read the fifth chapter of St. Matthew, and when I came to the end of it, you pointed out the passage concerning loving your enemies, and told me that our Saviour thought it no proof of heart-service if we only loved our friends, but that, to please Him, we must love, serve, and do good to those who were our enemies. I seem to hear your very words, and from that time to this I have loved even poor Kern, who was the only one who never loved me."

Aline was silent. She felt the farmer's strong frame tremble.

" Child," he said, " I, too, thought I had forgiven, until the serpent again crawled on my homestead."

" But that was not the forgiveness our Lord begs for. He must have all our heart, and you are His servant."

" I know—I know—' Out of the mouths of babes and sucklings.' Missey, you do not know what you ask. You did not know her—my Mary."

"Oh, daddy, he loved her dearly, but the temptations of money and rank were great. He repents so humbly : he would begin a new life with us elsewhere, but how can he go away, how can we go with him, with your curse heavy on our hearts ?"

Tears came into the old man's eyes, and he brushed them hastily away. Aline kissed his forehead, and leant her head on his.

"It may be very long before we meet again, dearest daddy ! It pains my heart to go away from this happy place, though I hope to return some day. But mamma cannot bear to have this strange story told while we are here, so we are going to London the day after to-morrow."

It was now Aline's turn to cry, and the farmer's to comfort. He put his arm round her waist, and said it would break his heart to part with her.

"I will come back," sobbed Aline, "but grant me this last favour before I go. See him and forgive him, once, only once."

"See him again I cannot, Aline. But if he be really thy father—if thee beest going

from us—if he be surely penitent—I will try
—God willing and helping—to—forgive—and
forget."

Aline's tears came faster and faster. She
could not speak. She put both her arms
round him, and he clasped her in both his,
and so the old man and the young girl, who
loved one another so dearly, bade each other
a silent farewell.

"God bless thee, and thy mother, and—thy
—father—" he said at last. "Take her, wife, go
with her, tell him from us both that we forgive
him for what he did to our Mary in heaven."

Again, and once again Aline kissed him,
then rising slowly, took Mrs. Bull's hand, and
led her out of the house.

"God forgive me as I do forgive him," said
the farmer, falling on his knees, and clasping
his hands.

Weeping and groaning he prayed long and
fervently. When he rose from his knees he
was calm.

"Christian's last burden cast away at last!
Maybe I ought to tell him so myself."

He went into the barton, where he saw
Jack and Joan gazing at something.

"Which way did your missus and missey go, glowbasons?" he said.

"Thickey way, measter.   Joan and I beant 'a courtin, we be a greetin.   Her did zay t' oi, her war a gwain awây, but her wouldn't forget t' wedding present.   There now, don't 'ee cry zo, Joan.   Her zaid as her'd come back. Now don't 'ee go vor to make your eyes zo red, my dear.   I can't abide to zee 'ee cry zo."

As Mr. Bull hastened on, Jack took Joan's hand, and comforted her by a very hearty kiss, and then they went their ways.

Mr. Bull met his wife coming home, and she told him that Aline and her father were gone across the meadows.   She, too, was crying. He made a short cut over the brook, and met them.

"William Eagles," he began impetuously, "this child tells me you are her father. Thank God for such a daughter.   She, and God's grace, have conquered my enmity against you. An hour ago I hated you with a deadly hate. I am now come to tell you that I forgive you on one condition.   You have sin enough on your head, let me ask you, first, if you are penitent."

"So penitent," said William, half humbly, half haughtily, "that I do not even feel angry at this unexpected sermon from your wife and you."

"Stop, daddy, hear him," said Aline, as farmer Bull was turning away.

"Yes, hear me, before you tell me the condition on which this tardy forgiveness rests. When last I asked for it, you left me for dead in your garden. Then I had just laid my wife on her bed, and left her in such agony of mind as I hope you may never feel. Since then I have been haunted by remorse, and, but for this child, should have destroyed myself. To find Mary in her quiet grave, and to know that her pure soul was in heaven — if heaven there be—was gentle suffering to that of finding my wife blind and unhappy, and knowing that I was the cause of both. And even this was peace of mind, compared with what preceded it. I believed myself the murderer of my wife. Not the slow villain that forsook your angel Mary, but the hasty villain that raised his hand against a woman. I tell you this to show you what I have had to bear. What demons have fought in my conscience, and how, as a Christian man, it is your duty to help me to subdue them. To forgive me unconditionally, so that, for the sake of my wife and child, I may not go mad, as I thought I should. Do not suppose that I can ever be happy, but I may be calm and penitent, as, I am told, was the Prodigal in the parable whom his father welcomed, as mine welcomed me."

"William Eagles, I *will* forgive you, unconditionally, but I will tell you what the condition was. That if you again forsook or ill-treated your wife or child, I would withdraw my forgiveness, and an old man's curse should once more rest upon your head."

Aline clung shuddering to her father, and said, "Oh daddy, how very dreadful!" William put his arm round her, and looking into Mr. Bull's face, said solemnly—

"I swear before God, here, beneath this vast temple of heaven, to you, its aged priest, that I will love and cherish till death this child and her mother, so mercifully restored to me, and will receive as my just due your curse if ever I break my oath."

"Then may God forgive you as I do!" said

farmer Bull, holding out his hand, which William took.

They stood for a few seconds, hand grasped in hand, and Aline put their clasped hands in hers, as if to ratify still more strongly the solemn compact. Then Mr. Bull walked hastily away, and left the father and child to pursue their course.

They went silently on by the babbling brook, till they came to the path that led to the church. William spoke first.

"Go on to the Nest, my Aline, while I ratify my oath at Mary's grave."

Aline would have combated this, but her father prevented her, by walking so hastily up the path, that she could not keep up with him. She did his bidding, and went to the Nest.

Agitated and exhausted, it was a relief to her to see Mr. Eagles quietly digging in his pretty garden. His white hair, and the white chrysanthemums, seemed to Aline emblems of peace. While she goes with him into the house, and tells the tale we have now heard, perhaps too often, we will see what changes the last twelve years have wrought in "The Eagles' Nest."

Mr. Oliver Bat has worked upon his cousins, the Misses Daw, to whom it belongs, to give him a lease of the house, and it has been his and Ellen's pleasure to add to its comfort and utility. A pretty little conservatory adorns one side, and the whilom schoolroom behind, is being converted into a sort of country institute, suggested by the utilitarian Lachlan. His ever-increasing "specimens" are already arranged in it, and it bids fair to become a good museum.

Mr. Oliver's great difficulty had been to persuade his father-in-law to give up his school. He could not bear the notion of a life of uselessness and dependence. The railway, so obnoxious to the Misses Daw, the working of chalk-pits, and the search for minerals, opened by Lachlan, had caused a new village to spring up on the other side of Yeo, about a quarter of a mile from the Nest, which was inhabited by navvies and mechanics of various grades. For their benefit Lachlan had frequently borrowed the school-room, and had lectured and taught, as was his custom wherever he went. Mr. Raven had assisted, and by degrees, the other gentlemen of the neighbourhood had joined, so that science, literature, and music, were making their way into that sturdy little aristocratic agricultural, and consequently behind-the-world village of Yeo.

Mr. Oliver took a great interest in the movement, and was getting up a library and reading-room, and adding another room to the school-room, for the purpose. It had taken a great deal of cunning argument on his and Ellen's part, to persuade Mr. Eagles that he would be of much greater use as librarian, secretary, and general manager of this institution, than as schoolmaster to country boys; and it had needed still more subtle reasoning to persuade him to receive payment for the office, but they had at last succeeded, and Mr. Eagles found his new post very much to his taste, and generally useful. His old age was gliding happily by amid books, flowers, and friends; and certainly if anything could add to his content, it was the unexpected knowledge that his misanthropic, melancholy son was the father of Aline, and, in his new relations, likely to be happier and better than he had ever been before.

While we have been discussing these little matters, William Eagles has joined his father and child in the parlour, and again poured out his penitence before the paternal tribunal.

CHAPTER XII.

"THE FIRST GRIEF."

DOUBTLESS my readers think, that after the *dénouement* of the last chapters, we ought to marry Lachlan and Aline, and have done with them. But many things happened, and several years passed, before that consummation took place. After a week's visit at the Lodge, Mr. and Mrs. Bat accompanied their relations to the nearest railway station, — where they were joined by Lachlan,—and saw all four off for London.

As I have resolved, in this tale, to fetter myself by keeping the "unities," I do not mean to follow them, but to continue where Aline would wish to be, at Yeo, or in its neighbourhood.

In the course of time, Ellen heard from her

brother and Aline, and the letters were satisfactory. They had taken a house in St. John's Wood, which, Aline said, "made-believe to be a country place;" and William was beginning to paint with a purpose. Mrs. Eagles was in better health and spirits than she had been for many years, and Dr. Dove was attending her for her eyes. Mrs. Dove, Lachlan, Mark, and Luke had been to see them, but of Kern, Aline only heard that she was with Lady Nux, from whose house she was shortly to be married. They were expecting a visit from Mrs. Eagles's aunt, and Fluke was "in a state of great excitement."

Aline's letter was all sunshine, and if there was a shadow, she did not let it fall upon the Lodge.

Before the year was out, Mrs. Bat presented the Mr. Bats with an heir. It was almost impossible to say whether the father or uncles was the most delighted. Every imaginable nursery, playroom, schoolroom was suggested, and Mr. Bat senior again plunged into brick and mortar, in spite of the laughing remonstrances of Oliver.

"I was just thinking," he said to Nicholas,

"that we ought to have made some sort of will, but now it will all, naturally, go to the boy —except what you, Nick, may like to leave Lachlan. I hope he'll be fond of farming."

"And fishing!" interrupted Nicholas.

"After all it was better that you and I never married, for then the property must have been divided; and Ellen is a capital housekeeper."

All sorts of little caps and boots came from Mrs. Eagles and Aline, who said, in the accompanying letter, that "her papa declared he had nothing to give, but that he would paint the baby's picture, as soon as he was worth painting." Fluke sent a knitted cotton counterpane, lined with pink, with her duty.

The following spring brought Lachlan to Yeo. Having made the estimate of Lord Yeominster's bridge, road, &c., and received due commands to undertake the work, he returned to the country to set about it. He was obliged to live at Yeominster, but frequently came to see his friends, and to act the steward for the Misses Daw, in whose favour he rose daily. He had somewhat sunk in that of Mr. Markman, by declining to go to Russia.

When at Yeo he took up his abode, as usual, at his uncle's, and was pained to see the alteration in him, and the evident carelessness he showed in all matters of business. He could not help fearing that death or ruin, or both, stared him in the face. His wife aggravated the evils by constant complaints, and Lachlan tried, in vain, to mend matters. He believed that Kern's marriage had been the crowning point of his uncle's trouble, and that the evident determination she had shown to have none of her family present at it, had worked upon his mind to the enfeebling of his body. One day his uncle verified his fears by confiding in him.

"You see, Lachlan," he said, "I was never born to be a farmer. That old taint of the baronetcy was in me, and I wanted to be something else. But I fell in love with Rhoda for her beauty, married, and settled down. Her temper, and ten children, have done for me. I shan't live long! I can no longer joke about the 'patience of Job' even—for if I ever had any patience, it is gone, and my patriarchal namesake was a better man than I. Lachlan, tell me about Kern."

"Uncle, I know little more than you do," said Lachlan. "I have not seen her since her marriage. I went, at your request, to the church, and saw her married. It was all very grand, and she looked like a queen. The Earl——"

"My son-in-law!" said Mr. Lyons.

"Yes—he looked dignified and happy. Sir John Nux gave her away. How he could have done it, I don't know; but I suppose his love, like his other feelings, was not very deep."

"Did Kern look happy?"

"She looked much as usual. Quite composed, and as if she had been married at least fifty times before. Everybody was in raptures at her beauty, grace, dignity, elegance, and what not."

"I suppose you saw 'The Morning Post?'"

"No, I did not."

"She sent it to me. Although she ignores us publicly, she doesn't quite give us up. There was enough of flattery to turn any woman's head—but her part of it was, that she was daughter of J. Lyons, Esq., of the Manor, Yeo; and niece of Sir Richard Lyons, Bart. You see, there was no lie in it. She simply left out two letters of my Christian name, and the word *farm*—and the rest sounded highly respectable.”

“I hope you parted from her in kindness ?”

“We had some words, but my pride being as great as hers, I told her that I didn't want to force myself upon Lord Inncaster ; and since she chose to marry a man who was ashamed of her relations, she must take the consequences of losing their affection. I am afraid she didn't care much for that. But I was so proud and fond of her, that her neglect of us all has nearly broken my heart.”

“But she has written to you ?”

“Yes ; and to Kezia. You saw ‘the Countess’ all through the letters. She said her husband would be happy to get the boys into some Government appointment or other. She wrote from the North, where my *son-in-law's* place is, as they call it. The only thing that has pleased me in it is, that it has delighted Rhoda, and put her into better spirits. A woman can find pleasure in crowing over her fellow women, that's a comfort. But I am afraid Kern isn't happy.”

"I think she is," said Lachlan. "She would have been miserable in an inferior position, and she is sure to please her husband and his family. Her tact is perfect."

A few months after this conversation, when Lachlan was again at Yeo, his uncle was seriously ill. He saw well that his days were numbered. He had another private interview with him.

"Lachlan," he said, "I have made you my sole executor. Not that I have anything to leave behind me but trouble. My affairs are in confusion. I am in debt and difficulty, but I believe there will be enough to pay every body, and leave a trifle for Rhoda. But her father will take care of her. You have such a head for business, that you'll put everything straight."

"I will do my best, uncle."

"I know you will. It was a good day for us when you came to England, though we didn't treat you very well."

"You made me one of your own children, uncle, and I thank you with all my heart."

"Rhoda has a kind heart, only it was always so wrapped up in her 'little angels.'

Poor Rhoda! I dare say she'll be better off without me. I was never good for much, and that was because I fancied I was too good for my place. You're the first Lyons who has done any credit to the family, that I ever heard of—and that was because you weren't above beginning from the very dirt and stones, as a navvy. Through you, my boys are getting on, and I dare say you'll have the title some day. But I shan't live to see it."

"My dear uncle — you talk as if you thought—— "

"I was going to die—and so I am. I hope my heavenly state is better than my earthly. I have been all my life trying to keep my soul in a sort of order. I have never neglected church, and the poor were always welcome. to a part of what I had. You don't think I'm far wrong, do you ?"

"I hope not, my dear uncle ; but I do not think it is any good to trust in our own righteousness."

"Thank God, I never did that. I have been such a poor, careless body all my life— spoiling my children, and ruining myself—that I should indeed be a fool to trust in any of my own doings. Be sure, my boy, I have but one only hope, and that is in the Saviour who died for all."

Lachlan bent his head reverently, and thanked God in his heart.

"Now I want you to write to the boys and Kern. They must all know my state, and come and see me if they will. I don't suppose Kern will come, but you must write, and tell her that I wish to see her before I go where Lord Inncaster and her father, Job Lyons, will, maybe, be side by side as equals."

"Could not Kezia write to Kern? I will write to the rest."

"No, you must do this last good office. Your words would have the most power. She thinks highly of you."

Lachlan did his uncle's bidding, and gave Kern his message, word for word. She was in London he knew, and therefore would receive the letter soon. Not that there appeared to be any immediate danger. Mr. Lyons was simply failing, getting weaker and weaker, but his wife and children scarcely suspected that he was gradually sinking from before their eyes.

"Don't frighten the boys," she said to Lachlan. "Job was always tall and thin and weakly. He's only poorly, and all the wine you've brought—I must say you're a good nephew, and more than repay what we did for you—will soon set him up. There's no getting him to take care of himself, and he with ten children—dear angels! I wish Matthew was here. Kern can't come. How can she, and she a countess, and so much to do, and grand people to see all day long? But I do think she might have had Mark and Luke and sister Dove to her wedding, though perhaps Lady Nux didn't wish it."

"They did ask Dr. and Mrs. Dove, aunt, but they declined, because Mark was not asked also."

"They were right. There isn't a genteeler young man in London than our Mark. But then lords and ladies can't do everything."

To the astonishment of the whole country, Kern arrived at Yeo the very day after she had received Lachlan's letter. She and her brothers came by the same train; but she being in a first, and they in a second class carriage, they did not meet until they got out upon the platform at the Yeominster station.

A fly and post-horses were awaiting Kern. She saw her brothers, and beckoned them to her. Somewhat against their lordly young wills they obeyed her commands, and got into the fly with her; and so they arrived at the Manor Farm at about eight o'clock at night.

It is not usual for countesses to visit country houses and country people such as the Manor and their inmates, even though they belong to the same; and the commotion caused by Kern's arrival was great. At first her own mother scarcely knew how to receive her; but Kern was only a shade more stately as Countess of Inncaster than she had been as the beautiful and ambitious Kern Lyons. She touched the foreheads of her mother and sisters with her lips, greeted Lachlan with a cold shake of the hand, and hurried on to her father.

He was seated in his old place, in the carved oak chair, in the chimney corner. The chilliness of illness made him need a fire, although it was summer, and the cheerful blaze kindled his pale face into something approaching the hue of health.

Kern had expected to find him in his bed, dying; but Mr. Lyons would not remain in bed, and staggered down, daily, to his accustomed seats—the sofa in the parlour, or the arm-chair aforesaid.

" You are not so ill after all, father," said Kern, kissing him with some appearance of natural affection. " Why did they frighten me so dreadfully ?"

She glanced round reproachfully; but Lachlan, for whom the look was intended, had disappeared.

" It was my wish, Kern," said Mr. Lyons. " Thank God, my dear boys, that I see you once more," he added, as Mark and Luke advanced, with grave faces, to their father's side.

" He'll get well again, now we be all here," said George Low, who never had conquered his English grammar. " You didn't see me, Kern. I suppose you haven't lost your memory with your name."

Kern turned round and shook hands with George.

"Kern, I am glad you came," said her father; "and you will be glad of it one of these days. Now I must go to bed. I can't sit up longer. Where's Lachlan? he helps me best."

"Lachlan's gone, father-law," said George. " We'll do just as well."

George and the boys helped their father upstairs; and then Kern was aware how weak he really was. Mrs. Lyons and Jemima were already busy preparing the best room for Kern, but Kezia was in attendance on her father.

Kern was left alone for a few moments, standing by the fire. Her eyes followed the melancholy party as they walked very slowly across the room, all helping, or seeming to help the dying man. At last tears came into those still enigmatical eyes, and she sat down in the chair her father had quitted, and cried silently, covering her face with her hands.

In spite of her acquired station, her beauty, elegance, talents, attire, that dying man was her father, and those were her brothers and sisters. Her natural feelings, such as they were, clung to them; the artificial ones to a higher sphere.

Had her conduct hastened her father's end? This was the thought that came into her mind.

Lachlan entered the room with Rhoda, who had been to fetch him when she heard her father ask for him. He gazed for a moment on the beautiful creature before him, sitting in the shadow of the chimney corner, with the flames from the big logs flickering about her, and suddenly remembered that first evening when he and she sat side by side in that same spot, surrounded by happy faces, all eagerly attentive to his stories of Australian life. How far away, and yet how near, seemed that day! And had it been his fault that he could not love her best?

She looked up when she heard his footstep, and seeing that he was about to withdraw, said, imperatively, "Lachlan, come here. Rhoda, ask Kezia to come to me if she can."

Both obeyed.

"Do you think he is really dying?" she said to Lachan.

"I do not know. He is very, very ill."

"You do not think I have done it?"

"Not all—certainly not all."

"You mean that I have helped. It was not my fault. It was not *my* fault."

Here Kezia and some of the young men came in, and the former took Kern upstairs. She told Rhoda to get the tea at once; and when the sisters were left alone together, the Countess threw herself into the arms of the humble Kezia and wept.

Scarcely had she time to swallow a cup of tea, and to take off her travelling apparel, before she was summoned to her father. They were alone together for a long time. We will not penetrate the sad mysteries of that last interview.

There was no sleep for any one in the house that night. The clergyman and the doctor both came and went. The former had administered the Holy Communion the previous day; the latter could do no good.

Mr. and Mrs. Bull came in the course of the evening; but everyone was soon so engrossed by the one thought—of death, that even Kern was unnoticed by them, save by a passing kiss.

The first sunbeams that penetrated the sick-room fell upon a sad, yet not altogether a hopeless scene. A soul was passing away, and a large family of children, wife and parents, were on their knees. Sobs were repressed with difficulty, as Lachlan read the prayer for the dying, and commended his uncle's soul into the keeping of the God who gave it. That uncle's last words had been words of faith and hope in his Redeemer; he had solemnly blessed his children, and prayed for the one absent son, present to him at that hour.

As the early summer sun rose brightly upon the vale, the church bell tolled slowly and mournfully, and the inhabitants of Yeo learned thereby that a good friend and kind neighbour had gone from amongst them; and knew that a widow and ten children were left behind to weep, and to find out what a husband and father they had lost, when he was too surely " no more seen."

CHAPTER XIII.

THE COUNTESS OF INNCASTER.

IMPERATIVE business obliged Lachlan to leave the next morning, and all the time that he could give his bereaved relatives was robbed from his hours of sleep. He managed to be with them the day of the funeral, and to join the long procession of children and relations who followed Mr. Lyons to the grave. Mrs. Lyons and Kern were the only ones who remained at home while he was buried. The former was unable to control her feelings, and the latter stayed, ostensibly, to be with her mother.

During those few sad days everybody seemed to forget Kern's rank, and she herself appeared to ignore it. Either a sense of duty, or a wish not to appear unfeeling in the eyes of the world, kept her at Yeo, but daily letters from the Earl urged her return to London.

After all was over, she became again the Countess, both in her own resolve, and in the estimation of all about her. The old haughty reserve returned, and she demanded and obtained, imperceptibly, the homage she thought her due. The only people she had seen beside her own family were Mr. Raven and his sister, and they yielded her, quite naturally, all that she desired.

When she heard that Lachlan was executor, she requested a private interview with him. He went to her in the parlour, and found her, in state, awaiting him.

"My poor father told me that my mother would be badly off," she began; "I am requested by Lord Inncaster to say that he will be happy to make any provision for her that you think proper."

"It is very good of his lordship," said Lachlan.

"If you will communicate with him on the subject; or, no—perhaps you had better tell me what you think would be sufficient."

"It will require time for consideration."

"I must leave to-morrow. Lord Inncaster is to meet me, and I should like to assure him that this matter is settled. I promised my father——" Kern's lip quivered slightly.

"I have been thinking of everything, Lady Inncaster," said Lachlan, whose pride was roused, in spite of himself, by Kern's manner, which was extremely haughty—but at the title, the lip quivered still more. "It is certain that my poor aunt will be obliged to leave this house, and Mr. and Mrs. Bull have already proposed that she and the girls shall go and live with them at the Downs. John declares his intention of giving up Australia for the present, and helping his grandfather, and we can easily dispose of Jacob and Esau."

"I wish they had other names. Lord Inncaster will procure them situations under Government. But my mother—what sum will she require to make her independent? All that Lord Inncaster requests is, that no one of the name of Lyons shall be allowed to want."

"*Want* would be out of the question as long as your mother's sons and I have arms to work. I *could* not name a sum, and I think your brothers *would* not."

"Then I suppose I may venture to suggest a hundred a year," said Kern. "I would see that it was regularly paid as long as my mother remains at the Downs. She proposed, yesterday, honouring *us* with her company : I need not say such a proceeding would be out of the question."

The lip, so lately quivering, curled.

"Oh Kern !" said Lachlan, involuntarily.

"You forget, Sir Lachlan Lyons, that I am Countess of Inncaster."

"Then your ladyship will probably allow me to terminate this interview. I will tell my aunt of your kind intentions."

"And the conditions appended ?"

"*That* I leave to the Countess of Inncaster !" Kern bit her lip.

"One word more," she said; "I have not been unmindful of you. I have set inquiries on foot at the Heralds' Office, and I find the old baronetcy may be resumed without much difficulty. A few preliminaries, and your early ambition, like mine, will be gratified."

"I have ceased to crave rank, unless I can earn and support it," said Lachlan.

"But I am resolved that *my* family shall be

known and respected. Your name is already inserted in the pedigree of the Lyons', and you are known as Sir Lachlan by all whom I now call relations and connections."

Lachlan looked annoyed.

" You probably consider this unwarrantable interference," said the Countess. " But I resolve that you shall at least owe me the gift of rank. Whether you will or no, you are considered the head of *my* family, and known as one of the oldest baronets in England. Neither pains nor money shall be wanting to complete the work on our parts. The Countess of Inncaster must have family as well as beauty and talent, to present to her husband's kin. Neither openly nor covertly shall they dare to say she was raised from the yeomanry to a coronet."

"The Countess of Inncaster has no right to take my affairs into her hands," began Lachlan.

"Right or no right, you *are* a Baronet, and henceforth you are known as such in the circles where I, alone, care that you should be known. Whenever you choose to renew Lord Inncaster's acquaintance, he will be glad to see you."

There was in Kern's manner, a something that even Lachlan could not understand. The haughtiness seemed to cover a sense of injury, which every now and then appeared in a tone or look. The last words sounded almost natural, and Lachlan said :

"I am a bad dissembler, so you must let me speak as I used to speak to you. I thank you for all the good you would wish to do me, and doubtless you have a right to cause your family pedigree to be drawn, and to put me in it. But I am a hard-working engineer, and have not money enough to support my title. Do not suppose that I have forgotten my poor father's last wish, that I should retrieve the fallen honour of the Lyonses. When I have made my way in my profession, and earned money commensurate therewith, I will come out as the veritable Sir Lachlan Lyons. But I would rather be the first of the name, and earn the title, too, by some such work as made Brunel a Baronet."

"And be the youngest Baronet in the country, built up by brick and mortar, or iron railway lines?" said Kern.

"Yes. And a much more honourable distinction than that of following some Norman, Danish, Saxon, or even Roman captain, to overturn old Britain, and her Christian faith, by fire and sword."

"Nevertheless you are Sir Lachlan Lyons, and I believe we have traced the first Baronet back to Caractacus or Boadicea, or some such antique."

Lachlan laughed, and Kern condescended to smile.

"You are a wonderful girl, Cousin Kern," said Lachlan, quite forgetting her rank, for the moment.

"You think so *at last*," said Kern, rising majestically from her seat in the old mullioned window, and giving Lachlan a look that made his eyes seek the ground in confusion and a sort of sorrow. It was a glance of such proud reproach that it was impossible to misunderstand it.

She was sweeping across the room, when Lachlan was impelled to say—

"Before you go back again to all the grandeur of your position, forgive my asking you one question, dear cousin. It is for my own comfort, and you will answer me, if only for the sake of our childish friendship. Are you happy?"

"I am perfectly happy, Sir Lachlan. I have

everything that the proudest woman in England could desire. You will be so good as to remember that I leave to-morrow, and wish to know what my mother says."

The Countess of Inncaster left the room, and Lachlan sat down in that same embrasure, which had doubtless often been the seat of her ancestors and his when in their prosperity, to think of her and them.

Subsequently Lachlan spoke to his aunt and elder cousins upon the subject of the annuity. Poor Mrs. Lyons began to cry at once. She had done little else since her husband's death.

"I am sure the Earl, my son-in-law, is very kind," she moaned; "and Kern is much better than I thought she would be, I must say that. A hundred a year's a very pretty bit of money, and more than poor Job and I ever had, to say clear, in all our lives."

"We don't want the money," said Mark and Luke, instinctively, together. "We'll work for mother."

"My dear angels!" sobbed Mrs. Lyons.

"But remember that you must work for yourselves first, boys," said Lachlan. "Mark,

you are scarcely out of leading-strings yet, and
Luke, you don't earn enough to keep you.'

That was true enough. Dr. Dove supplied
the one, and Lachlan, in part, supported the
other.

"Besides," said Kezia, "Kern is mother's
child as well as we are. She has as good a
right to help her as we have. If she can afford
the money, Rhoda and I will do the work, and
make granny and mother comfortable, while
John helps grandfather. We have no right to
exclude Kern from her part. She told me that
poor father said he forgave her any trouble she
might ever have caused him, and hoped she
would help mother."

Here they all began to cry together.

"Kern has a good heart," sobbed Mrs.
Lyons. "Tell her, Lachlan, I'm much obliged
to her, and to my son-in-law, the Earl, and by-
and-by I shall hope to take a turn to the
North, or to London, and see them. It will
do me good to have a change of air, and new
scenes."

Kezia saved Lachlan the trouble of the
addenda, and said, glancing at him—

"There will be time enough to think of that,

mother; but I am pretty sure that neither granny nor we shall ever let you out of our sight. I think you may venture to tell Kern that, cousin."

"Dear angels that you are! I'm sure I ought to be thankful for such children. If only Matthew was here. I suppose Australia would be too far for me to go and see him and his wife and children! I shall have nothing to do, now Job's gone—poor dear!—but to think of my weak health, and there's nothing like change of air for that. A hundred a year would take me to my son-in-law the Earl's, and to Matthew's too, I dare say. But I don't think I shall last long after your father."

"We will take care of you at home, mother. Tell Kern, cousin, that I will answer for all she wishes," said the good and prudent Kezia.

"But I don't see why I need leave this house at all," said Mrs. Lyons. "Why can't we go on here?"

"My uncle directs that everything shall be sold, and the debts paid," said Lachlan, "and says that John is not old enough to manage this large farm, so it must be given up."

"Then why did you send away Matthew?"

"Mother," said Kezia, "Mrs. Eagles and Aline have given granny nearly all their beautiful furniture. You will have her parlour, and be better off than you could be here."

"Her parlour! Well, that will be nice. Why it's better furnished than Mrs. Love's or the Miss Daw's drawing-room, with a sofa, and easy chair, and everything comfortable. If Kern and my son-in-law the Earl were to come down, we might receive them there quite genteelly—or sister Dove and the doctor."

Lachlan now considered that matter settled, and told Kern so in the course of the evening. He was not alone with her again, but she said to him curtly, that she would tell Lord Inncaster, and that she was sure that the annuity would be regularly paid.

It may be as well to say here that Lord Inncaster did pay it, and that the first quarter was sent to Lachlan in advance as soon as Kern arrived at home.

It could scarcely be said who felt the most relieved at the departure of the Countess of Inncaster from the Manor Farm—that lady herself, or her affectionate relations. The restraint on all sides was very irksome. Kezia was the only one who seemed not to feel it, and with her the Countess was at her ease. She would very soon have quarrelled with her mother, and Jemima and George openly expressed their wish that she had never come. The younger ones were afraid of her, and Lachlan and she, during their rare interviews, were, as we have seen, at cross purposes. Still it fell to his lot to go with her to the Yeominster station, and see her off.

Either by design or chance, she chose the same day for her departure, which Lachlan had fixed on to go to Lord Yeominster's on business, and naturally she offered him a seat in her carriage. She had managed to remain at Yeo until Mark and Luke were fairly in London—this was, also, either by design or chance.

Poor Mrs. Lyons wept as usual on the morning of her departure, but Kern shed no tears. She was truly thankful to get away.

"You will write to me sometimes, Kezia," she said, as she kissed her favourite sister with some slight appearance of affection.

"Provided you answer my letters," said Kezia, gravely.

"Give my love and—and—duty to my son

in-law," sobbed Mrs. Lyons, as the very best carriage and pair possessed by the Yeominster Arms drove off.

"Lor, mother," exclaimed Jemima, "what do you fret and bother for? She's glad enough to go away, and hopes she will never see us any more."

Kern was just ejaculating similar sentiments.

"Thank heaven that is over!" she said, as Lachlan, at her request, went inside the carriage, and took his seat opposite her. "My poor father and Kezia are the only ones of that family with a drop of the pure Lyons' blood in them—the rest are Bulls, indeed, by nature if not by name. Now, Sir Lachlan, I wish slightly to improve on the conversation we had the other evening. If there is anything Lord Inncaster can do for any of them to forward their prospects in life, and—to keep them at a respectful distance, will you let me know? I imagine all you have to say about filial and sisterly affection; but you know I never had much except for my father and Kezia, and they were the only ones who cared for me. Still, the twins with those frightful names, may be educated into gentlemen, and we would try to bring about so desirable an end. Unless you marry, Matthew will be the next baronet, and the others his younger brothers—so we must try to raise the family. Again I say apply to me if you want interest or money. And if you are not too proud, I might assist you also. One request of mine would do more for you than years of toil, believe it. I am not Countess of Inncaster as a lay figure, I assure you. *I* wrote to Lord Yeominster about the bridge."

Lachlan felt much annoyed, and Kern saw it, and rejoiced.

" After all you will owe title and position to me! You shall, at least, be grateful."

" You would greatly oblige me if you would let the title alone ;" said Lachlan ; " and for the rest I can work for myself."

"Oh! I shall amuse myself in my own manner. Remember that I helped you to build up your first museum. Surely you do not grudge me this little additional pleasure !"

" Cousin Kern, I shall never forget all your old kindness, but I would rather make my own way in life, without getting by interest what I do not deserve."

" 'That is what you will not do, Sir Lachlan. If any unexpected piece of good fortune befals you, think of me. Now I wish to explain to you one or two things that must have puzzled you. I was married from Lady Nux's, instead of from Dr. Dove's, at Sir John's especial request. He had the peculiarly sentimental wish to give me away to another, if I would not have him myself. That was *his* pride. We all have our pride—mine of rank, yours of independence, his of the opinion of the world. He did not wish anybody to suppose that I had refused him, or that he was broken-hearted. Poor little butterfly! broken-winged would have been the better expression. So Lady Nux crowned her many favours by a wedding breakfast, and Sir John by acting as father. Both are more than repaid by having the entrée at ' Inncaster's,' as Sir John calls my husband. We did ask Dr. and Mrs. Dove, because a family physician is always a respectable person. We did *not* ask Mark and Luke, because they would have been more uncomfortable than I should. Fancy them sitting on the edge of their chairs, and saying sir and ma'am and my lord and my lady at every word."

"Mark and Luke are very nice, gentleman-like fellows," said Lachlan, "and nobody need be ashamed of them."

"They are improving. I mean to get Luke an army-surgeonship in the Guards—and you and I will push on Mark. I am sure you cannot say that I neglect any of my relations."

Kern was now so entirely her old ironical self, that Lachlan could say nothing. He could only listen.

"And the Earl will do anything that I ask him. He is the most yielding of men. Quite unlike you, Sir Lachlan."

"I wish you would call me Lachlan, Cousin Kern, at least till we get out of the carriage."

"Provided you do not call me *cousin*. I always hate that addition. And so, the meek-eyed Aline has turned into an eagle, and flown to London. That was even more romantic than my marrying an Earl."

This was the first time that Kern had named Aline, and her face flushed as she did so Lachlan's flushed also, for he thought of his stormy interview with Kern, which she was resolved to bury among the bones of the past.

"When are you going to make her your wife?"

" As soon as she will consent to become so," said Lachlan, looking out of one window, while his cousin looked out of another.

" To-morrow then, I suppose!" said Kern, sarcastically.

" I fear I must have to wait for many a to-morrow. Aline will not leave her parents, and they will not part with her. I am the victim, and must wait and hope."

Lachlan sighed as he said these words. Kern was silent, and her face again turned pale. Each looked out of the respective window, until the horses suddenly stopped near the Yeominster station.

The train was there, and there was no time to lose.

" Lord Inncaster and a servant will meet me at Dorchester—they came with me so far," said Kern, "I did not choose them to come farther."

Kern was in the carriage when she said this —Lachlan held out his hand, saying—

"Good-bye, Kern. Believe that I am grateful for your good will, and will do what you wish. May you be happy!"

"We are friends once more," whispered Kern, returning the pressure of his hand, then added aloud, "Good-bye, Sir Lachlan Lyons. We shall hope soon to see you at Inncaster."

There were two ladies and three gentlemen in the carriage, all Dorsetshire people, who heard the adieu.

"That must be the Countess of Inncaster," they whispered to one another; and Kern was content.

CHAPTER XIV.

OUR GRAND-NEPHEW, SIR LACHLAN LYONS.

THE next thing which Lachlan had to do in his first hour of leisure was to call on his great aunts. They received him almost affectionately. They inquired for Mrs. Lyons and her family, which at once enabled Lachlan to begin upon the subject of his visit. This was to ask if the ladies would generously take the Manor Farm off the hands of Mrs. Lyons, without a whole twelvemonth's notice.

"My aunt is left badly off," said Lachlan, "and I scarcely know how she will be able to pay the arrears of rent, much less the whole of another year."

"Your uncle was an improvident man, and a careless farmer," said Miss Daw. "A true

Lyons. There was never one of them good for anything."

" He was kind and generous," said Lachlan ; "but he had a large family, and his health was not good."

" We must have given him notice to quit, had he not died," said Miss Daw.

" We certainly must," said Miss Ann.

" Then you will not mind, perhaps, taking up the house ?"

" On one condition," said Miss Daw. " We have made up our minds, so we may relieve you of your anxiety. We have a good opinion —I may say a high opinion, sisters—of you."

" A high opinion," said Miss Ann.

" We are very fond of him indeed," said Miss Harriet.

Lachlan bowed. Miss Daw continued.

" We never make promises, but this we may say, that if your conduct continues such as it has been, we shall—we shall—not forget you."

" Not forget you," echoed Miss Ann.

" I shall always remember you, nephew," said Harriet, emboldened by seeing the lengths her seniors were going.

Lachlan bowed again and again. Miss Daw resumed:

" With regard to the Manor, we have determined to take it off Mrs. Lyons's hands, and put it into yours. We are so much gratified by the improvement of our property under your management, even in this short time, that we wish you to take it entirely under your care, and to reside at the Manor."

Lachlan looked surprised, and said, " You are very good, and I am greatly obliged, but my profession will not admit of my settling down, even if my means would."

" I think we have provided against that contingency—eh, sisters ?"

" That contingency," said Miss Ann.

" We wish you to make the Manor your home, going and coming as suits your profession, which will evidently keep you principally in this county for some time. Cousin Bat tells us that there are several public works,—those abominations of desolation, railroads—bridges, docks—what else, sisters ?"

" Fortifications — piers,—lighthouses —tunnels."

" Oh ! I remember ; and aqueducts, viaducts

—far preferable to those abysses of evil, tunnels,—irrigations, of which I wholly approve —and various other scientific proceedings, of which you are sure to get the management."

" Mr. Bat is too good a prophet to be a true one," laughed Lachlan.

" Not at all. Ever since those two little affairs, the rooks—you remember ?"

" The poor, dear rooks! We can scarcely number them now!" said Miss Ann.

" And the fearful adventure at the Royal Oak — we have prophesied your success — and we will not forget; but we never make promises. So we wish you to make the Manor your head-quarters, and in your leisure hours to see to our property."

" But, ladies, the whole of my time would be required to work your farm properly ; and I cannot give up my profession."

Miss Daw and Miss Ann waved their hands majestically, one after the other.

" We propose to let the land separate from the house, until you settle down in life. We wish the word farm to be disconnected with that of Manor; and shall have pleasure in still seeing a Lyons in the home of his ancestors. Perhaps when we—but we never make promises."

" Never make promises," said the Echo.

"We mean to improve the house; and think that a clever and scientific man like you will be able to restore it to its old condition, by refreshing the out-buildings,—now turned into sheds,—repairing the panelling, carving, and so on."

"Oh !" broke in Lachlan, his eyes beaming with intelligence and pleasure, "that is what I have wished to do ever since the first night of my arrival at Yeo."

" Precisely," said Miss Daw.

" Precisely," said Miss Ann.

"I have the plan perfect, both on paper and in my head. The Manor, as it originally was, must have been lovely. The drive and entrance at the side, where the cart-road now is; terraces and lawns sloping down to the river; the hedges thrown down between the three large fields to the east; and those fine old elms freed from underwood. All plaster and whitewash removed from the wood and stone-work; and the kitchen and fruit gardens turned into a flower-garden. What could be prettier ?"

"Nothing. You have described it just as my grandfather used to tell us that he remembered it in his youth. And we would restore it, to a certain extent. Will you undertake it ?"

"Gladly, if time and money were at my disposal; but——"

"You can do it by degrees; Rome, you know, was not built in a day."

"Nor London, sister !" said Miss Ann.

"And we have accumulated money that may be profitably spent in this way. You can live in the house, as it is, free of rent, as— our grand-nephew, in short."

"Our grand-nephew !"

These last words were uttered by the old ladies with effort and effect, and were intended to astonish Lachlan ; which they did.

Miss Harriet ventured to take his hand, and to say—

"There ! now it is all out, and we mean to look upon you as a relation; so do call us aunts, my dear."

"Aunts ! It seems so strange !" began

Lachlan, slightly bewildered; but recollecting himself, continued: "You are really very good. I am most sensible of your kindness; but I must have some time to consider this proposal, as it must involve my giving up distant work, and therewith some of the fame I seek."

"We are not indifferent to your honour," said Miss Daw, stiffly. "And it is our opinion, that, although this new trade of engineering may be very respectable, it is but a trade, after all; and a country gentleman, living at his ancestors' manor, is very far superior. Besides, we look forward to your resuming your title in the course of a few years; and—and— but we make no promises, sisters,—we make no promises."

"We make no promises," said Miss Ann.

"I am sure I should be glad to promise everything," said Miss Harriet. "He saved our lives, and the poor dear rooks."

"Hush, my dear. You are so impetuous!" said Miss Daw.

Lachlan could think of nothing but of the ambition of women. Here were his old aunts and his young cousin, all hankering after that obsolete title. And he, too, began to feel the old ambition spring up again. Then he thought that he should like to make his Aline Lady Lyons. It sounded well, even in the mute language of thought. It would sound better still outspoken. Where, he asked himself, the next minute, were his resolutions to earn back the title by the fame of an Isambard Brunel, or not to take it at all? Perhaps, after all, it was wiser to receive thankfully the good things that came in one's way, than to let them slip while waiting for better.

"One other little matter, *nephew*," again began Miss Daw, with a stress on the latter word, which made Miss Harriet exclaim, "That's right, dear sister!" "We take it for granted that you, like other young men, think of matrimony. It is only when we come to ripe years of discretion, that we acknowledge the superiority of the single state. Cousin Bats and ourselves are examples. But with regard to matrimony, we should wish you to look high; if—but we make no promises."

Echo: "No promises."

"Neither do I, my dear *aunts*," said Lachlan, with a stress on the last word, which caused Miss Harriet to exclaim, "That's right, you dear boy." "I should really wish to oblige you, if I can, in all you have proposed for me, thus far; but in the matter of marriage, I shall oblige no one but myself, and, I hope, my wife."

"So like his unfortunate mother," said Miss Daw.

"His unfortunate mother!" said Miss Ann.

"The dear creature! We all loved her, sisters; and that is why we can't help loving Lachlan."

"I should never have cared for him but for his own merits, my dear Harriet," said Miss Daw. "As regards marriage, nephew. You see what a wonderful step in life that extraordinary young woman, your cousin, has made. And no one can say it is above her, for she has always shown herself a genuine Lyons, of the old stock, and is unequalled in beauty and accomplishments. We prophesied this when we first met her at the Vicarage. Could not you follow her example? I do not insist on money, but a lady of family."

"As you seem really interested in me, as I

know you were in my poor mother ——"
said Lachlan.

"We brought her and Mrs. Love up,—our
eldest sister's children,—left orphans at an
early age, from an imprudent marriage. You
see with what reason we dread matrimony."

"On account of this kind interest, I will
tell you that I am already engaged to be
married!"

"Engaged!" said all the ladies at once.
"And so young!"

"I shall soon be thirty; and I am not
likely to marry for some years."

"That is well. You will change, if the
match is not suitable, in the course of years.
Long engagements never come to anything."

"I hope he will never change!" said Miss
Harriet, emphatically. "She is a sweet creature!"

"You know, and have never told us!" said
Miss Daw.

"Never told us!" echoed Miss Ann.

"I was not certain—am not certain," stammered Miss Harriet.

"It is scarcely a secret," said Lachlan;
"and you are all welcome to it, as far as I am

concerned. For *her* sake I do not wish it talked about. I have been engaged to Miss Eagles for some time."

"Humph!" said Miss Daw, stiffly.

"Miss Eagles?" said Miss Ann, interrogatively, not at first comprehending who he meant.

"Miss Rambully, sister," said Miss Harriet; "that sweet little girl of whom cousins Bat are so fond; and who reconciled her parents, and used to visit the poor; and has left a name behind her that will never die. I remember you once said she was really like a violet."

"A sweet, but *humble* flower," said Miss Daw. "But there are many worse. Tell us who they really are, Lachlan. I am told the mother was a woman of condition."

"Mrs. Eagles is the daughter of the late Sir Thomas Sedgland, of Sedglands Abbey. The present baronet is her first cousin. I know him slightly. I believe he has been to see Mrs. Eagles in London; and their aunt, Miss Auster, is with her now."

"Then they have forgiven this misalliance. The world is full of misalliances, I declare," said Miss Daw.

"Yes. She was her own mistress when she married; and now they are very glad to have found her again. She and Mr. Eagles and Aline are invited to Sedglands Abbey."

"But William Eagles is like an Italian bandit," said Miss Daw.

"Like some one in the 'Castle of Otranto,'" said Miss Ann.

"But he is a great man, nevertheless," said Lachlan. "He has this spring been elected a Royal Academician, and is one of the first painters in the world. He is to have a thousand pounds for his next picture, if he will only paint it."

"I look upon a professional painter as little superior to a painter and glazier," said Miss Daw.

"What do you say to Sir Thomas Lawrence, and Sir Edwin Landseer?" asked Lachlan.

"That they have no right to be Baronets. I certainly consider either of your cousins to have a much better right."

Lachlan laughed.

"Then, if I recovered my title as a reward for engineering ——'

"Don't name it!" cried Miss Daw, uplifting

her hands in horror, as did Miss Ann. "I should prefer spending any sum of money to recover it in the direct line of ancestry—but we make no promises. However, as regards Miss Eagles, I consider her to belong simply to the Sedgland family. Her father was a mistake, found out too late, and as such, must be tolerated. Sisters, we should see no great objection to that sweet young person?"

"No great objection!" said Miss Ann.

"I shall love her dearly, and if she comes to the Manor I shall go and see her every day," said Miss Harriet.

Lachlan's colour rose, and his heart beat quick, at that charming idea of Miss Harriet's.

"As regards the Manor," resumed Miss Daw, "you know that it was originally the seat of your family. Then the village road did not go near it, and the fields to the left were part of the grounds. But as the family sank lower and lower, and the property was sold piecemeal, the Manor House became the Manor Farm, the road was cut through the grounds, and my father, and the old Sir John Nux, got, by degrees, the principal part of the property into their hands. But this was when there were few remains of its manorial grandeur, for it was all cut up into farms and dairies. I have every hope that you will, in the course of time, be able to purchase back some of it. Meanwhile, the Manor House, being ours, and untenanted, we will begin by restoring that. Now we will have tea. Sister, ring for tea. It is past nine o'clock."

"You will have the advantage of our rookery," said Miss Ann.

Lachlan did his best to make himself agreeable to the old ladies, and succeeded. He told them he would consider all they had said to him, and see them again in a few days. He left them immediately after tea, and had the honour of kissing the cheeks of the two elder ladies, and really embracing the younger,—an honour, I am sorry to say, he was not as ambitious of as of the title.

When he got into the moonlight of that summer evening, he tried to make out what it all meant, but failing, he went off, at a rapid pace, to the Downs Lodge.

He found the quartette playing whist, Ellen and Nicholas being partners. He heard Nicholas mildly assuring Ellen that she had lost the odd trick, and Oliver declaring that if he were Nick, he would not have such a partner.

"Bless my soul, what brings you here?" said Mr. Bat, as Lachlan entered.

"Take my hand, Lachlan, do, and finish the game," entreated Ellen. "I want to run away, I do indeed."

"That confounded young rogue of a baby," said Mr. Bat.

"He pulled off Oliver's spectacles to-day!" said Nicholas, "and——"

"And nearly all my remaining grey hairs," said Mr. Bat.

"Do take my cards," again said Ellen.

Lachlan took them at once, while Ellen went to look at her baby, and he and Nicholas won the game.

When it was finished, Lachlan told them of his conversation with his aunts, and asked them what it all meant.

"It seems pretty clear," said Oliver; "the old ladies are going to make you their heir, and this is how they are training you."

"But what am I to do?"

"Stick to them like a leech. Wipe their shoes, and sweep their garden, and help build the rooks' nests if necessary, but don't offend or contradict them for the world. They are not very young."

"And if you want a few hundreds—" whispered Nicholas.

"And Aline—" said Mr. Bat.

"You can have them," said Oliver. "There is no better woman of business in the country than Cousin Margery. You began your conquest with the rooks, and finished it with a drive—not to Gretna; and now she has planned all this business to be executed by you."

"I wish you joy with all my heart," said Mr. Bat senior. "But you'll have hard work for some years. You'll have not only to build the Manor up again, but Lord Yeominster's bridge, and all the public works in the county. I hear your name wherever I go, in connection with some project or other."

Here Ellen returned, and the tale was told to her again.

"It will all come right at last," she said; "I knew it would. What a happy family party we shall be!"

"With the children dancing, dancing on our knee!" responded Oliver.

"Let's have another bottle of that old port, and drink Lachlan's health," said Mr. Bat.

"Then you think I ought to take up my abode at the Manor—and give up London?" said Lachlan.

"You certainly ought to make the Manor head-quarters, and keep an office in London," said Oliver.

Lachlan thought of Aline, so did Ellen.

"We will get them all down here," she said, "and make them give up Aline."

"She is more necessary to her parents than ever," said Lachlan.

"Do they quarrel?" asked Ellen, anxiously.

"No. Aline is always near to prevent even a recrimination. If your brother stays too long at his easel, and poor Mrs. Eagles is annoyed, Aline runs to fetch him down. If her mother is irritable, and her father excitable, she soothes the one and calms the other. She is an angel."

"Is she happy?"

"As the day. Cheerful as a bird. And Fluke is a great comfort to her, and pets and scolds her as of old."

"Are my brother and his wife happy?"

" How could they be otherwise, with Aline ?
And even without her they would, I think, be
happy ; but Aline does not think so. Fluke
says they agree like lovers—quarrel and make
it up—and bill and coo like two old turtles.
She is very amusing, and likes London much
better than the country."

" How many rivals have you, Lachlan ?"
asked Mr. Bat.

" There are half a dozen painters, and as
many authors, and her cousin, Sir George, and
poor Luke, constant as ever, all raving about
her. Sir John Nux has found them out, too,
and is quite devoted."

" The fickle swain !" said Ellen.

" But still she is constant to her one engineer ?" said Oliver.

" She says so."

" Here comes the port. We will drink
Aline's health as well," said Mr. Bat.

While doing so, that worthy man did not
forget to tell Lachlan that if he could be of any
use to poor Mrs. Lyons and her family, he
would gladly be so. They also advised him
not to refuse any offers of service that Lord

and Lady Inncaster might make, and to get the boys placed out as soon as possible.

Lachlan left the Downs Lodge late, to return to the Manor, where he found Kezia and John waiting up for him. He told them, in part, what the Misses Daw had said; and, after they had separated for the night, he sat long meditating upon what he ought to do in this momentous crisis of his life. He ended his meditations by resolving to do what seemed to be his duty, as day succeeded day, and to leave the result to Him who ordereth all things well. It appeared clear to him that, as long as he was professionally employed in Dorsetshire, he might manage to undertake the improvements and renovations that his aunts desired to make in the Manor, and to divide his time between Yeominster and Yeo, so as to please all parties. But he felt that what with public and private duties, he would have quite enough upon his hands.

CHAPTER XV.

THE RETURN TO YEO.

THE Misses Daw behaved very kindly to Mrs. Lyons and her family, and allowed them to remain at the Manor as long as was convenient. But by the autumn, stock and crop were all sold, with such parts of the household furniture as could not be conveniently stowed away at the Downs Farm or Brooklands, or bought in by the Misses Daw and Lachlan for furnishing his apartments in the old house. Poor Mrs. Lyons cried a great deal when she left the Manor, and Kezia was very sad; but they were at once so comfortably settled with Mr. and Mrs. Bull, that the change could scarcely be called an unhappy one. As the old people were well off, and as their eldest daughter,

Mrs. Dove, was also amply provided for, there was no one to object to the arrangement.

John consented to remain with them for some time, but with a view of ultimately joining his brother Matthew in Australia. Jacob and Esau were sent, as boarders, to a neighbouring grammar-school, whence, Lachlan hoped, their sister, the Countess, would get them drafted into something better. He had had one or two formal letters from the Earl, in which his lordship gave him to understand that he would assist in the education of the young people, provided they were not, personally, intruded upon him until he chose to receive them. Kern was in the zenith of her power.

One of the first things that Lachlan did, when he was fairly installed into his own rooms at the Manor, was to send for Stern. This worthy old man had been working as a navvy up to this period; but Lachlan, knowing his honesty and shrewdness, put him into the office of overseer of the works at Yeominster, and felt that, by so doing, all would go on during his absence as during his presence. He also gave Mark engineering work under himself; and thus secured two allies in the business.

This enabled him to give more time to the re-
novation of the Manor, in which labour, also,
he found friends to assist, to whose intervention
his aunts made no objection. These were Mr.
Eagles, who had a great taste for landscape
gardening, and old oak carving as well, and
Mr. Bat, who was well pleased to be allowed
to see to the farming part of the affair. Thus
Lachlan's friends, made by his own merits,
turned to good account in his time of need, as
all friends deservedly gained always do.

These changes made a great impression on
the good people of Yeo. Various were the
surmises as to what the Misses Daw meant to
do for Lachlan, but it was generally supposed
he would be their heir. The old ladies became
quite brisk, and were busied from morning to
night in walking from the Rookery to the
Manor, making their observations and giving
their orders, and then walking back again.

Captain and Mrs. Love were naturally much
annoyed, and saw that all Bob's prospects were
over. But their aunts were still as kind as
ever to them and Margaret Anne, so they did
not relinquish their hopes of succeeding to the
inheritance themselves. They perceived that

their best policy was to be civil to Lachlan, so they invited him frequently to dinner—more frequently than he cared to go—and made Margaret Anne sing her prettiest songs for his benefit. But Lachlan was invulnerable to all the arts of all the syrens of the country; even though he could seldom find time to see Aline, and when he did she was as obstinate as ever in her resolve not to marry *at present*. In vain he reasoned, and lectured, and grew angry; she only laughed, and said they were both quite young enough to wait—years younger than Mr. and Mrs. Oliver Bat were when they married—and that she could not leave her parents.

Three or four years passed in this way. The Yeominster bridge and road were finished, to the great approbation of Lord Yeominster, and to the considerable increase of Lachlan's income. Important works were offered to him in different parts of the country, and he bid fair to be a rich man as well as a celebrated engineer. Lord Yeominster had taken him fairly by the hand, and invariably gave him his title; and he was now more generally called Sir Lachlan than Mr. Lyons. This, he believed, was due to Lady Inncaster, as Lord Yeominster had once said that his lovely cousin, the Countess, had told him his history. Half the world supposed he was knighted for some engineering work or other; the other half knew that he was a Baronet by right, and so his early ambition was accomplishing.

Meanwhile the Manor went steadily on, and Lachlan saw the ancient abode of his ancestors gradually resume its primitive beauty and respectability. Granaries became handsome rooms, with carved ceilings, and panelled wainscots—cheese-lofts turned into bedrooms and morning-rooms that overlooked the rich Vale of Marchmoor—kitchens resumed their old state as dining-rooms; and back-kitchens and dairies became kitchens and servants' hall. This was truly a labour of love to Lachlan, and a labour of great interest to his friends.

When it was nearly completed he asked his aunts if he might be allowed to rent it of them. He told them that his income was now so good, and his prospects were so bright, that he could do so, provided the farm were still let separate. They were delighted at the proposal, consulted him as to the proper rent, and let him have it at a third of the sum he named. He was quite in the zenith of their favour. He took possession of it, and of course he furnished it by degrees, with a view to his Aline's being some day its occupant.

Mrs. Bat wrote constantly to Mrs. Eagles and Aline, to entreat them to come and pay her and old Mr. Eagles a visit. The reply she always received was, that Mrs. Eagles was still under Dr. Dove's care, and that when a pending operation had been performed on her eyes, and that she could safely leave London, she would certainly go to the Downs and the Nest. As to Aline, she could not leave her mother, and William could not leave them.

About six years after William Eagles, his wife and child left the Downs, Ellen wrote to beg they would make up their minds to come, as her father's health was failing, and she feared that if they delayed much longer they might not see him alive.

To this letter there came an affirmative answer. The operation had been successfully performed, and Mrs. Eagles' sight, although not perfect, was much improved. It was Aline who wrote, and her pen could, evidently, not run fast enough to express the joy she felt at returning to her dearly-beloved friends.

"Mamma," she said, "wishes to go to the Nest first, because she has got used to small rooms, and thinks those darling little snuggeries will just suit her. She never saw the Nest, you know. Indeed she never *saw* any of the dear old places, but now she will be able to verify the truth of my powers of description. Oh! the great blessing of feeling that she can at least see, in part, the objects around her. When we meet, dear aunt, I shall be able to give you some idea of the operation. It was very good of Dr. Dove to let me be present. I do not think either mamma or I could have borne it, if I had been out of the room. She has been much more cheerful and composed since it took place, and does not dread going back to the Downs as much as she did. I only wish she and papa would settle there. He paints too closely, and Dr. Dove says he will injure his health, and bring on another attack upon the lungs, if he continues to do so. But when we are all together once more we will make a regular onslaught upon them.

You and I will lead on the Mr. Bats, grand-father, and Lachlan: and I do not think they will resist us. Tell the latter forlorn swain that I heard Sir Lachlan Lyons mentioned the other day, as having written some wonderful article in the 'People's Magazine,' upon 'Institutes,' and 'Popular Lectures.' I thought of that Australian lecture in the dear old schoolroom, and of our first meeting at the Royal Oak. I see him now, sitting on his big box of specimens, and myself pulling his coat-tails. Hurrah! for the Royal Oak. We shall all be there again in a day or two."

And there they all were, and thither my readers must accompany me to meet them. Twenty years have passed since we first saw them under that wide-spreading tree, and it does not require much philosophy to observe that many are the changes wrought in that space of time.

In spite of the Misses Daw, the inn is, virtually, if not nominally, a railway inn, for the Royal Oak station is close at hand, and such passengers as need a night's lodging— and very few they are—go to Mr. Tunny. That excellent landlord does not find his busi-

ness much improved—on the contrary, he says
the old posting and stage-coach days were far
the best—but he is obliged to go with the
stream. He keeps a refreshment-stall at the
station, and has a stray engineer to lodge with
him ; but, for the rest, he now depends on the
alcoholic element.

The train arrives at six o'clock, and Mr.
Oliver Bat has considerately given into Lachlan's charge, his pretty britschka and pair of
greys, on condition that Aline shall sit on the
box beside him. Lachlan is at the Royal
Oak exactly at five minutes before six, and
awaits the train on the small platform, while
Mr. Tunny holds the greys. There he finds
Mr. Bull.

" I couldn't be happy without a first sight of
her, Sir Lachlan," said the farmer.

"Call me Lachlan, granfer, or we shall
quarrel. You and I were both here when
she came down first, nearly twenty years
ago."

" Yes, my lad, and I thank God I am spared
to see her again. I didn't venture to say I
was coming, or they'd all have wanted to
come. I suppose you *will* get married now ?"

"It depends on her. Talking of marriages; I was so glad to see John Dull and Joan so happy in your shepherd's house the other day. They showed me Aline's present, and were looking forward to seeing her as much as any one."

" We are all looking forward to it. But I must tell you a bit of a secret. Kezia has had an offer. It came by letter, and took us all by surprise. Do you remember Mr. Horsfall, the architect of the Downs Hall ? A very sensible, superior man. It seems he always had a fancy for her, but couldn't marry before."

" And Kezia ?"

" Says she can't leave us—but I don't think she is indifferent; and now Rhoda's growing up to take her place, I hope she'll marry and make a home for herself."

The whistle of the train interrupted Lachlan's comments. Mr. Bull withdrew into the little waiting-room.

In a few minutes Lachlan is actually kissing Aline ! Don't blush, ladies ! They are engaged, and Lachlan was always an adventurous young man. Now he is helping out Mrs.

Eagles, shaking hands with her husband and Fluke—seeing to the luggage with Aline by his side—and finally standing by it till the train again flies off.

"It is all so strange," says Aline, looking round. "Where is the Royal Oak? Daddy! my dear daddy!" she exclaims, seeing Mr. Bull peeping out of the waiting-room.

She runs towards him, shakes hands, puts up her face for the accustomed kiss, asks for granny, Mrs. Lyons, Kezia, every one in a breath. Says it is so kind—so very kind—of him to come and see her, and finally leads him to her mother.

"Lunnun hasn't spoilt thee, my darling," says farmer Bull, wiping his eyes.

Mrs. Eagles receives the old man quite affectionately, and he presses William Eagles' hand in token that bygones are, indeed, by-gones.

"You. drive off, and I'll see the luggage into the cart," he says to Lachlan.

Accordingly they go round to the Royal Oak, where Mr. Tunny awaits them.

"The horses are anxious to be off, Sir Lachlan; they are in good condition. The old ladies won't go by train, nothing can induce 'em. Glad to see you looking so much better, Mr. Eagles."

Lachlan blushes deeply at being called " Sir" before Aline, and hurries them into the carriage.

"How grand it sounds! I feel quite respectful!" laughs Aline, as she makes herself comfortable by Lachlan's side.

Only once does the undutiful girl turn round to her parents during the drive! But then, the wheels make such a noise that they could not hear what she says, and she knows that her father is pointing out to her mother, and describing, every object that they pass.

It is summer, and how beautiful everything is on a fair summer's evening! Lachlan can scarcely think of his greys for listening to Aline's exclamations of delight.

" Who would live in London when they can live in the fresh, pure, lovely country! Oh! look at the haymakers just going home from work! I must go and make hay at the Downs. You will come, Lachlan? Yes, and give up those horrid old plans for a breath of sweet hay. I never smelt a really naturally pleasant perfume all the time I was in London."

"And yet you will stay there, Aline!"

"I must, you know, you tiresome Lachlan, as long as papa and mamma do. Oh! look at that festoon of dog roses, twining with the honeysuckle. In all the world there can be nothing like these Dorsetshire roads."

"Certainly not for ruts and dirt in the winter. Do you remember how you used to trudge through them in pattens, and lose the pattens in the mud?"

"I delight in pattens. As the riddle says, 'They elevate, they extricate, they save.' There are the Downs! The dear, dear Downs! Now I am at home again."

Aline stood up in her excitement, and clapped her hands.

They were not long in reaching Yeo. At every cottage door within a mile of the village, women and children were out to see Aline. She knew them all, and bowed, and kissed her hand, and smiled to every one.

"There is Mary Martin with a new baby! and that must be the ex-baby holding her skirts! And there is old Mrs. Leech in the porch. She must be better. Stop, Lachlan! You must stop for Mr. and Miss Raven and dear Mary."

Lachlan obeyed orders, and cordial greetings were interchanged at the Vicarage gate.

"I suppose Captain and Mrs. Love are as grand as ever. I see nobody in their windows. But look, Lachlan! There are your aunts, the Misses Daw, all standing at the window, bowing to you. I must kiss my hand to the old ladies, I can't help it. How kindly they nodded and smiled at me! What a noise the rooks are making! Why, there must be a hundred at least."

"No, only eighty-seven, so my aunt Harriet told me the other day."

"Lachlan! Mamma! Papa! what place is this?"

And Aline turned round for the first time to her parents.

"All of this is mine and thine," whispered Lachlan.

Aline was too bewildered to make any remarks on the new old Manor House. Where she had left a farm, she found a handsome private house. The old entrance was gone, and a drive through what was once a barton wound round through some fine old elms, and was lost, she knew not where.

Lachlan watched her excited, inquiring face, as he drove slowly up the hill, and whispered again—

"You will not leave me in that grand old Manor alone—you will never go back again."

But Aline's black eyes were full of tears. Quickly they gathered and fell down her flushed cheeks. Lachlan suddenly remembered what she remembered. Poor Mr. Lyons and his ten boisterous children, and the welcome he gave Lachlan so many years ago!

Lachlan pressed her hand, and drove faster. They did not speak again until they reached the Nest, where old Mr. Eagles, and Mr. and Mrs. Bat, and their little son, were in waiting to receive them, attended by Jenny, now a buxom young woman.

The warm greeting on all sides may be well imagined. Mrs. Eagles walked up the path through the garden, leaning on her father-in-law's arm.

"This is an elysium," she said.

In truth it was a paradise of flowers and sweets; a nest in which all the song-birds of heaven seemed to have assembled in company, and upon which the pure air of the Downs blew its freshest breath.

A real country tea was awaiting them. Fresh eggs, fresh butter, fresh milk and cream, fresh fruits, fresh flowers—and cold chicken and ham, *ad libitum*. All the windows were open— all the birds sang a welcome home. Aline danced to their music. No sooner were her travelling things off, than she literally danced on the little green before the house, in her child-like mirth, and made her young cousin dance with her.

"Tired! how should I be tired?" she said, "Am I not come home again?"

While they are all at tea, we will just glance at the party, and see what changes six years have wrought in them. Mr. William Eagles still looks ill, but graver and calmer than he did. He watches his wife with an anxious attention, rendering almost unnecessary Aline's ever-ready care. That wife looks at least ten years younger than when we saw her last; more cheerful and happy, and far more healthful. The partial recovery of her sight has been indeed a boon to all, and she cannot apparently gaze enough on the friends by whom she is surrounded, in order to understand the countenances of those whom she has never seen before.

"You are all so different from what I had imagined," she said, involuntarily, when Mr. Oliver caught her eyes fixed on him. "Even Aline's graphic descriptions failed to give the expression. I recognise the features."

"Handsomer or uglier?" asked Oliver.

"Handsomer, of course."

Aline is but little changed. The same loving eyes—the same arch smile—the same trick of finding her little hand in that of her next neighbour. At this moment it is creeping into her grandfather's, who has been loading her plate with strawberries and cream.

"I want some, grandpapa," said a little jealous voice, and Ellen's black-eyed boy runs in through the open window, he having been left in the verandah to play with his nurse.

Aline soon coaxes him into her lap, and shares her strawberries and cream with him.

"Give uncle Lachlan some," was his cry, and Aline had soon two helpers.

"May I take a plate-full to Fluke?" she asked. "She is having her tea upstairs."

Permission granted, off flew Aline, and met Jenny on her way.

" Dear miss, now I be glad to zee 'ee," said Jenny. "I've been a moast dazed ever since you goed away. Old measter be so quiet, and Mrs. Oliver be growed zuch a grand lady, that there beant nobody to speak to."

" We'll have some fun, Jenny," said Aline.

" I often thinks o' thickey there letters, miss! he, he! and they to marry after all !"

Fluke was well pleased with the strawberries and cream.

" One need 'ave something to make up for coming into this out-o'-the-way place again. What you can see in it, Miss Aline, I caunt think. As to Jenny, she's duller than ever, and her eyes are bigger. But you're happy enough, I dare say."

" And you must be happy too, dear old Fluke," said Aline, " and dance the polka with me directly."

Whereupon Fluke was whirled round the room, till she laughed heartily, and so satisfied Aline.

At about half-past eight o'clock, Mr. and Mrs. Oliver prepared to walk home across the

Downs, their son having preceded them immediately after tea.

"I will put on my hat and go some way with you," said Aline.

"You will be tired to death—you must not, *carina*," said her father.

"She shall not go far. I will take care of her," interceded Lachlan, and off they went across the Downs.

They walked some way together, in lively converse, Aline's spirits being so much lighter than the air, that Lachlan declared that he was afraid she would be carried off: and then they separated, and the happy lovers loitered homewards.

They took no note of time, and when they came to the spot above the Manor House, they stopped and sat down upon the very stone on which George Low had tried to learn the capital cities years before.

The last rays of sunlight were fading over the vale and river beneath them, and a white mist was rising above the meadows. But over the Downs and the Manor, the moon shone in clear beauty. Her rays revealed the flower-beds, garden-paths, and shrubberies that now adorned the house, in the centre of which the old sun-dial still stood. Not a sound disturbed the peace of the scene. Even old Yeo and Max sat quietly at the feet of the happy pair, who, hand in hand, gazed silently on the ancestral home of Lachlan Lyons. At last he broke the silence.

'I have done it all for you, my Aline. If you will not share it with me, I shall go away to some distant occupation. I cannot live here alone. I think if you loved me in the same way that I love you, you could not resist me so long."

"Lachlan, you know my only reason. If papa and mamma could only do without me— if they would only settle near——"

"They are quite happy—you have smoothed away almost all the asperities. They live for one another now. You must see that they do, Aline."

Aline uttered a little sigh.

"I think they *are* happy, and I know they love one another—still there are times—if I could be near them, perhaps, if——"

"If they will consent, my Aline. May I ask them? May I just hear what they will say? Only think that I have loved you twenty years, and waited for you patiently nearly ten. They ought not to be so selfish as to part us longer. Only let me see what they will say?"

" But if you were to quarrel, I should be so unhappy. And now we are all so united. It is better to wait, Lachlan."

" Till we are old and grey. And for no reason whatever. I have a good house, a good income, good friends, a will and hands to work, and a heart to love and cherish you, Aline. Are you not bright and cold as that moon?"

Aline looked at him with eyes so loving and tender, that he knew the comparison was unjust.

" We should be very happy in that dear house," she said, simply, " if only they were near us."

" May I speak to them? You may at least grant me this little privilege, after ten years."

" If you like, Lachlan. But you will not quarrel about me?"

" No, my Aline. It must be, indeed, a heavy provocation that could make me do so. We shall be very, very happy."

CHAPTER XVI.

LACHLAN CARRIES THE PARENTAL FORT.

LACHLAN was obliged to leave Yeo the next morning at sunrise, and nearly a week passed before he was able to return, not until late the following Saturday night. Meanwhile Mr. and Mrs. Eagles settled down in the Nest, to Aline's perfect content. Old Mr. Eagles was soon better in health, under the cheerful influence of society, and seemed to lengthen his fast dwindling span of life in seeing that his son appeared to be beginning his anew under happier influences.

We have passed quickly over the last six years, because, as I said, I did not care to leave Yeo for London. But they did not fly so swiftly or with so slight consequences to William Eagles and his wife. They did not

all at once learn how to live tranquilly together. Passionate natures do not calm down in
a day—reserved natures do not become open
in a day. The seeds of pride and jealousy,
sown profusely in early life, will not root up
of their own accord, and the husband and wife
who have disagreed and separated at thirty, do
not become patterns of conjugal happiness when
they unite again at forty or fifty.

Therefore Aline was not altogether wrong
in believing that her presence had been essen-
tial to cement the union she had brought
about.

But six years had done their slow and sure
work. The husband and wife were sincere in
their desire to improve and make one another
happy, and if they could not do this at once
they did it by degrees. The return of love
was the chief aid, but it was not the only one.
Aline's " word in season," gentle and playful
ever, and never apparently said for any purpose, was the secondary help. She knew how
to turn a conversation that was beginning to
be unpleasant, or to introduce a mutually
agreeable subject when reserve was oppres-
sive. She could cast oil on the troubled

waters of her father's irritable temper, or flatter the little vanity of her mother when she fancied herself neglected.

At the end of six years, however, she began thankfully to find that her intervention was less and less needed. Her parents understood one another, and made excuses for mutual defects. The return of sight was the crowning blessing. William no longer so bitterly reproached himself with having caused the blindness of his wife ; and she felt that she could now enter into his pursuits, and was not so keenly alive to real or imaginary neglect. She could now see what he really meant from the expression of his face, instead of trying to understand by the variable tones of his voice.

There were great discussions at Yeo, and even in the neighbourhood, as to who would call on Mr. and Mrs. Eagles. The Ravens called of course, and were gladly received by both. Miss Daw, who was her own mistress, and never cared for what other people said or did, declared her intention of calling on Lachlan's account.

"I shall make a point of saying why I do so," she said, "or Mrs. Eagles may consider herself insulted, as we never noticed her at the Downs Farm.   But then, sisters, she was under a cloud——"

"Decidedly under a cloud," said Miss Ann.

"I should have said, under the Downs," said Miss Harriet.

"In the Downs would be more appropriate. But I do not wonder at any woman running away from William Eagles," said Miss Daw.

The Loves resolved to call because their aunts called.

"Though I'm sure I don't see why they called," said Mrs. Love. "Those Eagles are nobodies, though to be sure she is the daughter of a Baronet, and his sister married Cousin Oliver. I never could understand how it is that some people get on in the world, and others stick in the same place, or go down as fast as they can. There's that Lachlan—well, you're right, Captain Love, he *is* my nephew, and it wasn't my fault I didn't notice him when he first came back; 'twas only because aunts didn't, and now he's everything with aunts; and our poor Bob is nothing. And there's that Kern Lyons a Countess, and our Margaret

Anne resolved to marry young Perch, the doctor, in spite of us all; and you and I, Captain Love——"

"Are as good as any of 'em," growled the Captain; "and I'll never knock under to the old women again as long as I live. There it is again. I am obliged to knock under to this confounded gout, and that's enough by ——," and the Captain swore a round oath, which he was never backward in doing.

So Mrs. Eagles and Aline held levees all that week, and the general opinion of them was that they were ladies,—" thorough ladies." Several carriages drove up to the Nest, the inmates of which called " on account of the Bats, you know," and Jenny expressed her surprise in such unmeasured terms, that Fluke indignantly rebuked her.

"Why Mrs. Eagles was used to see more carriages in a week than Yeo sees in a year," she said; "and all the village, Captain Love's and the Manor included, would have gone into her father's park and looked like an egg in a field. Sir Thomas Sedgland would have bought up the whole vale."

"Lor! be he alive now?" asked Jenny.

"No, but his nephew is, and his son would be only too glad to marry Miss Aline if she'd have him."

"Oh, her be a gwaine to marry Sir Lachlans," said Jenny. "Volks do zay as how Madam Daws 'ull leave 'un everything. I hope zo with all my heart."

It was remarked by all the visitors that William Eagles did not make his appearance to any one; and as most of them had seen either his original paintings, or engravings of them, they were much disappointed. He had become a celebrity, but he would not show.

"I am not going to be patronized, *ma mie*," he had said, "by people who never showed me or mine any civility before we married into the 'county families.' Do not say '*Papa taci*,' *Alinetta mia*, for I hate the whole brood."

And so the Royal Academician had absented himself from the drawing-rooms held by his consort and her daughter.

Lachlan had made his friends at the Downs confidants, by letter, of his intended raid upon the old Eagles to carry off their young one, and Mr. and Mrs. Oliver had sounded the Nest.

"Lachlan and Aline are having quite a Jacob and Rachel courtship of it," said Oliver.

"I scarcely understand you," said Mrs. Eagles.

"They have been engaged so long," said Ellen.

"Engaged! scarcely engaged!" said Mrs. Eagles, whose eyes had been shut, literally, to the real state of the case. "They are like brother and sister; and Aline always says she will never leave us."

"But you surely do not suppose she wishes to die an old maid," said Oliver. "You would not wish that?"

"She is quite young. She is only—how old *is* Aline?"

"I declare the *fanciullina* is—name it not in Italy—twenty-eight years old. It is really time she should marry, *anima mia.*"

"It startles me," said Mrs. Eagles. "Time passes so swiftly that I had forgotten her age, and I always fancied that we could never live without Aline. Could you, my darling?"

Mr. Oliver Bat growled something aside. He always protested to Ellen that people who used such tender epithets in public, always fought in private.

Mr. Eagles senior entered at this point of the conversation, and took it up.

"I think you ought to let them marry. I should like to see them one before I die, and as Lachlan has taken to the Manor, we should be all close together. If you would only live here with me. Stay and close my eyes, William, and be near your child, and go to London when it is absolutely necessary. Ellen, light of my eyes! don't you think this might be accomplished?"

"I certainly do, my dear father."

"And we could get my admirable cousins Daw to build you a studio," said Oliver. "They have the taste of brick and mortar, and Mrs. Margery was saying, the other day, that she didn't know what they should do with themselves now the Manor House is finished. I told them that they had better break up the present road, and restore the old one, building a new entrance, where one was said to have been formerly."

"That was close to this house, you villain," said Mr. Eagles. "Why they say this was, generations back, the lodge ; and that the stone porch over the back door is intact."

" Well," said Oliver, " if William does not give them something else to do, the old ladies will end in making you Sir Lachlan's lodge-keeper."

" I should be very happy. But do let the young folks marry. My dear daughter-in-law cannot, I am sure, forget how hard it was to wait."

" It would have been better for her to have had a life-long courtship," said William, frowning at the allusion.

" I shall tell Lachlan to go in and win," said Mr. Oliver; " and if he is opposed, to carry her off bodily. I will get the licence, clergyman, and all ready."

During this conversation, Aline was at the Downs Farm, whither she had gone, laden with presents, to see her old friends. When Mr. and Mrs. Bat left, Mr. and Mrs. Eagles thus further discussed the subject.

" It seems impossible that she should be nearly thirty, William. In my sight she is still a child."

" To me, *carissima*, she is only ten; for I

have known her but ten years. Could we do without her? It would be like tearing out a tooth to part with her, but, when once over, we might, perchance, make up our minds to the loss."

"She says she does not wish to marry—that she means to live with us; this was the reason she gave her cousin, when he proposed, and poor disconsolate Luke also. But, to be sure, she is very much attached to Lachlan."

"Could you do without her, *ma mie?*"

"Could you, dearest?"

"*Ma bien aimée,*—I am afraid you would not be able to put up with me without Aline. My temper is still so irritable, and I am such an invalid."

"Your temper is perfect, and I can nurse you now."

"*Carina*, do you think I am less of a brute than I was? Say so again."

"You are no brute, my love. You are what I believed you to be when first I knew you."

"And you could live alone with me, without fear of your life, *idolo mio?*"

"Why do you say those horrible things? I

could live and die with, or for you, as I pray to do."

"Then I may try to forget the past, and get rid of the demons that haunt me?"

"I know of no past—I live only in the present, and hope for the future."

"Thank you, my wife! Then if you can be happy with me, as I can with you, we will let them marry, and may God bless them!"

"He will. Aline is sure to be happy. But, one word, William. If I seem cold or reserved again, promise not to think I am so to you. It may be pain, or a passing thought, or anything but you."

"I promise, *mon amie*. I promise."

William Eagles took his wife's hand, and then kissed her affectionately.

"God bless our child! It was all her doing —God bless her!"

Soon after this Aline returned.

"Darling, we have been talking of you," said her father.

"Thank you, papa. And I have been talking of you."

"Do you wish to leave us, *Alina mia?*"

Aline's cheek flushed, and her head drooped.

"Come and sit by me, Aline," said her mother, "and tell me honestly, whether it has been on our account, or your own, that you have remained with us so long?"

"Dear mamma——"

"Whatever you say, *carina*, you will not make us angry, or unhappy."

"On both, I think," faltered Aline.

"And now, would you leave us, or would you still remain with us?" said her mother.

"I will do—whichever you like," said Aline, very nearly breaking down.

"But you must do whichever you like, my darling," said her father. "We have made up our minds to be both good and happy without you; have we not, *ma mie?*"

"Yes, if Aline wishes it."

"Oh, papa! oh, mamma!" said Aline, hiding her head on her mother's shoulder. "Can you really do without me?"

"You proud little *mignonne*," said her father, seating himself on the other side of her, and putting his arm round her waist, "do you think no one can live without you, because Lachlan cannot?"

"But will you stay here, papa? I could not be happy far away from you?"

"Perhaps we may—but we will talk of this another day; *la cara madre* has had enough of it for the present. We must not have the *bel ciglio divenir lagrimoso.* You were our good angel and brought us together; let me be yours, and think that I give you to Lachlan, who deserves you if any one can. Is it so, *ma mie?*"

Mrs. Eagles put her arm round Aline, and burst into tears.

"Do not mind me. I cannot help it. We will live near you, my own darling, and see you every day."

And so, when Lachlan came to the Nest the following Sunday evening, he found the fort carried for him. William Eagles met him, and a very few words between them settled the whole affair. They went into the room in which Aline, her mother, and grandfather were sitting, and there sealed the compact, as such compacts ought to be sealed, by parental blessings, and inward prayers.

There were not, on the face of the earth, two happier beings than Lachlan Lyons, and his Aline.

CHAPTER XVII.

MISS DAW'S FIRST SPEECH.

THE wedding took place in the pleasant month of August. We must be old-fashioned, and end with the wedding, on account of one or two momentous events that occurred at it. Aline's ideas were so large that the Nest could not hold them, so she was obliged to be married from the Downs Lodge. She must have all her friends to see her married, by whom we are to understand the party from the Downs Farm, the family of Ravens, and her own and Lachlan's relations. Mark Lyons came from London, to act as groomsman, while Kezia and Rhoda, and two Miss Ravens were bridesmaids. Poor Luke could not come, and Mr. and Mrs. Bull and Mrs. Lyons declined being of the party at breakfast, but promised to go to church for the ceremony.

The sun shone brightly on the auspicious morning, upon arches of flowers, happy faces, and a crowded church and churchyard. And never was Hymen's torch kindled to lighten the path of a more joyful bridegroom and bride. Lachlan and Aline were truly one, in every thought of the heart; and firm and loyal,— frank and sweet were their voices, when they repeated the words that bound them together for life and death. Everybody said " God bless them," and all remarked that so trusting, bright, and happy a face as Aline's, had never before been seen beneath a bridal veil and wreath.

But it was at the breakfast that the event occurred which it concerns us to know. After the usual toasts and speeches, Miss Daw stood up, and declared her intention of making her " maiden speech." The information was received with great approval, and Mr. Bat said, " Now we shall have something worth hearing."

" As I see none present but relations, connexions, and intimate friends," she began, bowing in her stately way to all.

"Intimate friends," echoed Miss Ann, bowing also.

"My dear sister!" remonstrated Miss Daw, and proceeded.

"I venture to wish our nephew and niece, in our joint names, happiness and prosperity."

"Happiness and prosperity," murmured Miss Ann, who was whispering word for word after her sister.

"As yet we have made them no marriage present; but we preferred doing so in the presence of this happy party assembled for the occasion. We have narrowly watched the conduct of our nephew, Sir Lachlan Lyons, ever since his arrival in the country. We met him, at first, with suspicion and dislike. He removed these evil feelings by his gallant conduct in a little affair concerning our rooks."

"Our rooks!" broke in Miss Ann, unable to restrain her feelings.

"Sister! I dare say you are inclined to laugh at our love for these birds; but they were connected with our family, and, as I said before, Sir Lachlan saved them from destruction. They have prospered ever since. But more than this, he saved our lives; and this is

the greatest benefit one human being can confer
on another. Moreover he obliged us in the
matter of the railway ; and all this, my relations,
connexions, and friends, when we had shown
him no civility or kindness—purely, I take it,
out of Christian charity. He has shown himself a Lyons of the old stock, such an one as our
ancestors knew and doubtless venerated—
therefore we have revoked our determination
not to acknowledge his father's son, and have
made our will in his favour."

Here Miss Daw was interrupted by such a
vociferous cheer, that she was quite overcome,
and Miss Harriet wiped her eyes. Others of
the party were similarly affected, and Lachlan
got up and sat down more than once.

Miss Daw bowed and waved her hand as if
deprecating this demonstration. As soon as
she could obtain silence, she continued :

"I am an old woman, and my sisters are
not young, and we may not live very long;
but I wish it to be understood that we do this
to show our sense of the manly and upright
conduct of a born gentleman, and with the
desire of seeing, during our lives, how he will
conduct himself as a man of title and property.

The only condition appended to our wedding present is, that he and his wife be, henceforth, Sir Lachlan and Lady Lyons."

"Sir Lachlan and Lady Lyons," echoed Miss Ann, emphatically, bowing majestically to the pair.

Lachlan was about to speak.

"I know what you would say, nephew," continued Miss Daw, "you cannot give up your profession. We do not wish it. You will require it to keep up your position until our deaths, when such of our landed property will be yours as once belonged to your ancestors. In justice to ourselves, I must add that we have not forgotten our other niece, Mrs. Love—only as regards heirship, we prefer the scholar to the bully."

"The scholar to the bully," said Miss Ann.

Miss Daw opened a large reticule that she had been industriously carrying all the morning, and produced a parchment and a jewel-case. She went solemnly towards Lachlan, who rose, looking flushed and embarrassed.

" In the names of my sisters and myself I present you with this deed of gift,—to you and your heirs for ever, to have and to hold, as the Lyons did before you."

" A little more firmly, I hope," muttered Oliver.

" I do not know what to say, my dear aunt," began Lachlan, who looked so very uncomfortable, that Aline came to support him.

"*Say* nothing, nephew, but *Do*. 'Deeds not words' be your motto, as it has been hitherto."

"Deeds not words, nephew," said Miss Ann, who was standing by her sister, round whom, gradually, all the party had gathered.

Fluke, be it understood, was a privileged witness of every part of the day's proceedings, having nothing to do but to look on and observe.

". And to you, my new and dear niece," continued Miss Daw, "we offer these jewels. Some of them belonged to your husband's mother; others were destined for her, and the rest are our wedding gift."

Aline took the casket, but, unlike her husband, knew well what to do. With her eyes full of tears that gleamed like diamonds, she put her arms round Miss Daw's neck, and gave her the most affectionate kiss she had had for many a year.

"I am so very, very much obliged," she said, "and so glad that Lachlan has that dear old Manor House."

Then she kissed Miss Ann and Miss Harriet, whispering to the latter, in addition to renewed thanks, "I always loved you very much, and shall love you better than ever now."

"And I you, my dear," said that kind woman.

"Read the deed, Cousin Oliver," said Miss Daw, adjusting her cap, which Aline had slightly disarranged.

Oliver opened the parchment, and peering into it, through his spectacles, read over a deed of gift, which conveyed the Manor House, gardens, shrubberies, and some adjacent fields, to Sir Lachlan Lyons, Baronet, and his heirs for ever.

"Now, Lachlan, you lucky fellow," said Oliver, "make a speech. I am sadly disappointed, for I fully expected the Manor for myself and my heirs for ever. Cousins, you adore rather the rising than the setting sun."

"Ladies, you will allow me, as Aline's

mother, to thank you very much," said Mrs. Eagles. "I am, indeed, happy in thinking that she and Lachlan have such friends."

"And we," said Miss Daw, "in feeling that our nephew and heir has married into a family of rank similar to his own, and of commensurate liberality. Your aunt and yourself have acted nobly in the way of dowry."

"Nobly, we all say," said Miss Ann.

"You forgot the poor painter's last picture," said Oliver, "and the thousand pounds it gave."

"I beg your pardon, Mr. Eagles," said Miss Daw, bowing to William. She could not yet quite acknowledge him as a sprig of the baronetage.

"You must say something, Lachlan," said Mr. Bat, in a whisper.

"Give them a lecture on generosity," said Mr. Oliver.

"My dear, kind friends," said Lachlan at last, "this piece of good fortune, as unexpected as undeserved, has quite overcome me. I think of myself twenty years ago, as I entered this parish poor, and, for aught I knew, friend- less, in search of a home and food. I see myself now, crowned with every blessing that man can wish for. A wife, whom I have loved all those twenty years—the title I came, by my father's commands, to recover—the home in which his and my ancestors lived centuries ago—my poor mother's early benefactors and beloved aunts, become my benefactors—the best of friends and relations surrounding me— and the profession I love, giving me a position among men of learning and science. I think of all this with feelings of so mixed a nature, that I fail to realize it. A sense of my own want of desert, and of the great goodness of Almighty God, can, perhaps, best be expressed, by saying that to *Him alone*, the 'God of the fatherless,' all praise is due: and I pray Him to bless and reward those good friends, who have helped me in my struggles for an honest maintenance, and who at this moment surround me."

There had been no tears during the marriage ceremony, but they fell plentifully while Lachlan was making his little speech..

"One word more," said Miss Daw. "I shall wish to be present when my young relations return home."

"To welcome them back," said Miss Harriet, who had her arm round the bride's waist.

"One more toast," cried Mr. Bat, "in which I am sure every one will join with all their hearts—Our worthy cousins, the Misses Daw —and may they live long to see the young people happy for whom they have done so much."

It need scarcely be said that the wedding party drank this toast with all their hearts, and that the old ladies had risen high in the esteem of all present.

After the excitement had subdued, Fluke carried off Aline. Her first words were, when she had her all to herself, and was beginning to take off the veil—

"Now, my lady, you must put on your travelling dress. Thank 'eaven I can say 'my lady,' with a clear conscience, and in the light of day."

"You stupid old Fluke!" said Aline, kissing the faithful woman affectionately.

"I can fancy what a sight you'll be, when you and Sir Lachlan—how well it sounds—go rampaging about over all those Welsh mountains."

"You'll take care of mamma, my dear old Fluke," said Aline. "We shall not be long.

I can't think why we should go away at all. No mountains in the world can be like the Downs, and no people so dear as they are here. Even the Misses Daw, that we used to laugh at, are quite as good as the rest. And did not the old lady make a capital speech, and was not Lachlan's answer just what it should be? And could any house be nicer that the Manor?—only I wish poor Mr. Lyons had not lived there before us."

Aline looked almost as pretty in her simple travelling dress, as she did in her wedding veil, and when she and Lachlan drove away in the Downs Lodge carriage, they did not leave a heart behind them that was not overflowing with love and good wishes.

CONCLUSION.

MISS DAW'S LAST SPEECH.

ONE more scene, and my story closes. My readers must accompany me to the Manor House, and see what is going on there. Scarcely has the usual "moon"—doubtless of "honey" on the present occasion—circled the earth since the bride and bridegroom went away, and this evening they are expected back. The Misses Daw have again bestirred themselves, and, aided by Mrs. Eagles, and the indefatigable Fluke, have nearly filled the old house with guests. We will walk through the rooms.

In the large drawing-room are all the party from the Downs Lodge, the young heir inclusive; Mr. and Mrs. Eagles, and their father; Captain, Mrs. and Miss Love, who gave their aunts strong hints that they wished to be on friendly terms with their *relations*; and the Ravens.

This room is furnished in modern style, and has no antiquity about it, save the carved ceiling and the oriel windows. From the west window we look out in front upon the flower garden, full of geraniums, calceolareas, and other autumn flowers, with its sun-dial and thick box-hedge as of yore; through the arch in the hedge more flowers are visible, that fill another garden, stretching to the church. Beyond the church the Downs. From another window, facing the south, we see the terraces which Lachlan restored sloping down to the river, and the rich meadows and corn-fields of the Vale of Marchmoor beyond.

We go out into the large hall, with its polished and carved oak staircase, and, through a massive oak door, into the panelled dining-room. This room, my readers may remember, was the large hall, and common sitting-room of Mr. Job Lyons and his family. It has been simply revived. The massive oak chairs, table, and sideboard were here in those days, but were much defaced—now they are valuable antiquities turned to modern service. Walls and floor are of oak, the ceiling is even more elaborately carved than that of the drawing-room, and handsome crimson curtains give a cheerful glow to the whole. The huge chimney-corner is intact, and a fire of logs of wood blazes on the hearth, while plenty of good cheer covers the table.

Here are assembled the Misses Daw, Mr. and Mrs. Bull, Mrs. Lyons, and such of her children as are within reach, the Squoire, George Low, Jemima, and their children, a certain Mr. Horsfall, architect, and, to crown the party, Sir John Nux, who has just come down for the shooting.

From this fine old room we follow some of the young Lows, and Master Bat, who has come in search of them, into an inner room, which proves to be a library, in which all Lachlan's and Aline's books are neatly arranged, together with many new works, presents from various friends.

We return to the dining-room, because we have forgotten to look at the old family portraits which William Eagles has taken great pains to restore to some of their original freshness, from the dust of generations; also at a portrait of Mrs. Eagles, lately taken by William, as a surprise for Aline; also at one of William's fine original paintings, of a scene at Venice, intended as a gift to Lachlan.

But we must not linger, as the September sun reminds us that it is between six and seven o'clock, and the train reaches the Royal Oak at six.

Through another heavy oaken door, and into the passages that lead to the offices, we go into the servants' hall, a good substantial room, lately the best farm kitchen. Here rules Mrs. Fluke, in new silk gown and white ribbons; and near her is Lachlan's factotum, Stern, a stalwart man of advanced age. In the middle of the room is a long table, laid out for supper, and scattered round it are the tenants of the Misses Daw, and the possible embryo tenants of Sir Lachlan Lyons, Bart.

We leave this room and go into the kitchen, where are assembled a large party of poor people and their children, all friends of Lachlan and Aline. Amongst them appear conspicuous John and Joan Dull, and all the labourers of the Downs Farm. Here is another well-spread table.

Returning to the hall, we feel tempted to run up the broad staircase, and to peep into the bedrooms. One of these retains its old tapestry, and carved-oak bedstead, once the pride and terror of the young Lyonses, but the other rooms are more modern. Here is a pretty little sitting-room, evidently for Aline, and it looks across the meadows to the Downs Farm, and you see the smoke curling up from one of the chimneys. How well Lachlan knew Aline's heart when he selected that room for her! and how hard he must have worked, and how saving he must have been, to have furnished this pretty room, and all the old house so well!

Servants are running about everywhere, and they are everybody's servants. Jenny is active and consequential among them, belonging, as she does, to the family; but Fluke is the head and chief.

Now the bells strike up a merry peal, and there is a distant sound of music. The Yeo band, consisting of drums, fiddles, and clarionets, are evidently "welcoming the coming guests," and a welcome more noisy than musical it seems to be. We look out of the windows down towards Yeo, and see a carriage coming up the street. Soon wheels are heard close at hand, and in another minute we see the Misses Daws' chariot enter the new gates, and roll along under the great elms of the new old drive, and we rush down to watch Lachlan and Aline alight, amid the joyful barkings of the aged Yeo and Max, at the original entrance, a stone portico, till lately belonging to the dairy.

Aline is in her father and mother's arms by turns, and Lachlan is kissing his great aunts. These are the only people privileged to come into the hall.

Miss Daw has arranged the rest of the drama, and, followed by her sisters, leads the astonished young couple through the various rooms. We need scarcely remain to witness what we anticipate must come—cheers, greetings, embraces, jests, tears even, according to the humour of the individuals. Lachlan and Aline are excited and overjoyed. They thank their great aunts again and again, and are as happy as they deserve to be.

Miss Daw's speech was pretty much the same to all, as she and her sisters, accompanied them from one friend to another.

" We imagined this little surprise for a two-fold purpose, to please the young people, who have hearts to love their friends, and to show that we ourselves choose to acknowledge Sir Lachlan and Lady Lyons as our dear nephew and niece, and to welcome them to the home of their ancestors."

Tired or not tired, Lachlan and Aline had to sit at the top and bottom of their huge dining-table that evening, and to use hospitality to all their guests. If it was somewhat of a scramble, it was all the better fun. The Yeo band did duty in the servants' hall, while the good folks danced to their music, without finding fault with its harmony, and Lachlan, Aline, and their friends danced with them.

Miss Daw made another little speech at supper, which ended as follows, and with which we will wind up our book.

" And so you see, my relations, connexions, and friends, that after various vicissitudes, this very ancient family is reviving again, and under fine auspices. The Lyonses of old squandered their patrimony, and were obliged to leave it for another country. The Lyons of to-day comes from a far-off land to make his fortune by honest industry, finds friends, restores the abode of his forefathers, and sits at this table as Sir Lachlan Lyons, Baronet."

" Sir Lachlan Lyons, Baronet," echoed Miss Ann and Miss Harriet, and from dining-room to kitchen resounded the words—" Three cheers more for Sir Lachlan Lyons, Baronet, and his lady."

THE END.

www.ingramcontent.com/pod-product-compliance
Lightning Source LLC
Chambersburg PA
CBHW020930120726
47905CB00008B/2459